ALSO BY M. SCOTT PECK, M.D.

In Search of Stones
A Pilgrimage of Faith, Reason, and Discovery

Further Along the Road Less Traveled
The Unending Journey Towards Spiritual Growth

A World Waiting to Be Born
Civility Rediscovered

Meditations from the Road
Daily Reflections from The Road Less Traveled *and* The Different Drum

The Friendly Snowflake
A Fable of Faith, Love and Family

A Bed by the Window
A Novel of Mystery and Redemption

The Different Drum
Community Making and Peace

What Return Can I Make?
Dimensions of the Christian Experience
(republished as *Gifts for the Journey*)

People of the Lie
The Hope for Healing Human Evil

The Road Less Traveled
A New Psychology of Love, Traditional Values and Spiritual Growth

IN HEAVEN AS ON EARTH

In Heaven as on Earth

A Vision of the Afterlife

M. Scott Peck, M.D.

SIMON & SCHUSTER
A VIACOM COMPANY

First published in Great Britain by Simon & Schuster Ltd, 1996
A Viacom Company

Simon & Schuster Ltd
West Garden Place
Kendal Street
London W2 2AQ

Simon & Schuster of Australia Pty Ltd
Sydney

A CIP catalogue record for this book is available from the British Library.

ISBN 0-684-81807-8

Printed and bound in Great Britain by
Butler & Tanner Ltd, Frome and London

To Lily
Fellow Journeyman
and
Best Friend

ACKNOWLEDGMENTS

Visions do not arise ex nihilo. This vision has too many sources to mention in their entirety, but I would like to single out three for my special gratitude: C.S. Lewis for his vision of hell in *The Great Divorce*; the Roman Catholic Church for keeping the vision of Purgatory alive; and George Ritchie, M.D., who reported the most thorough and enthralling near-death experience I know in *Return from Tomorrow*, a report that helped inspire Dr. Raymond Moody to write *Life after Life*.

And writers do not exist ex nihilo. Like all other humans and creatures, we survive only because we live in what Charles Williams called a "web of exchange." From within this huge web I wish to express my appreciation to those members of my support system who have been most intimately involved in the production of this book: Jonathan Dolger, my agent, and Brian DeFiore, its editor and publisher, who discerned the worth of its first draft; Susan Poitras, our infinitely competent office manager, who typed that draft and its rewrites; Gail Puterbaugh, our program director, who insightfully pointed out the significance of "the green room"; Valerie Duffy, who tidies up after us; and Lily Peck, our general manager, to whom this book is dedicated.

Any book on the afterlife is inevitably a work of fiction. Hence the characters herein are fictional and not intended to represent any actual person in or from this life.

IN HEAVEN AS ON EARTH

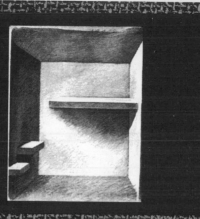

CHAPTER

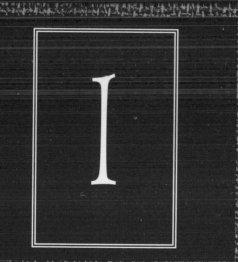

I knew the moment it happened. I'd been in a coma for two days. Now, instantly, I was somewhere near the ceiling of my bedroom. A body of an old man was lying in my bed. I could clearly see our daughter sitting to the right of the bed and our living son to the left. Both of them were crying softly. The body was waxy gray, and obviously dead. I knew it was mine but emotionally, as far as I was concerned, it was an it; it had no connection to me nor I any attachment to it.

I knew all about it. The cause of its death was cancer of the lung with multiple metastases to the brain. To the children's chagrin, I'd smoked my beloved cigarettes until the very time I slipped into coma. I felt sorry for them that they had to grieve. But then I'd spent much of my life feeling sorry for them; children have to bear so much pain.

Otherwise, I felt exultant. I'd been divorcing myself from life—life in the body on earth, that is—for over a decade, and most emphatically for the last three years since Mary Martha had died.

One piece of my exultation was scientific. The business of looking down from the ceiling in detachment was classical. So many accounts of near-death experiences had described this out-of-body moment exactly. Yet for those of us who'd not had the experience, their accounts represented a hypothesis. The scientist in me now had the joy of seeing a hypothesis, a theory, personally confirmed.

But my real joy was that it was finally over.

The joy was tinged with fear, however. These accounts were from those who'd returned from death—who'd been sent back. I desperately didn't want to be sent back. They'd also usually described a frightening next step of helplessly being whisked at great speed through a seemingly endless dark tunnel.

That step occurred almost as soon as I began to fear it. Only for me it was not a tunnel. Not quite. It reminded me of the times in my youth that I'd been seriously drunk and had what were called the "bed whirls"—brief times when alcohol had deadened my inner ear, the balance apparatus, and the whole room would nauseatingly spin about me. But now there was no room. And it was dark. Black. I'd totally lost my moorings. It felt as if the cells of my body had all become unglued, which I suppose, in a way, they had.

I was just starting to become terrified that this sickening sensation of being completely lost in space might last for an eternity when the light oriented me. It grew very slowly closer. The reports of near-death experiences had often identified it as Christ or God. My own first reaction to it was simple gratitude for the sense of orientation it restored to me.

Then, closer still, I had a strong feeling that it was beckoning. Finally, I was sucked gently inside of it. The light was neither blue nor white, silver nor gold. It was unidentifiable. What was so extraordinary about it was the sense of acceptance with which it received me. Never had I felt so accepted.

Long before the reports of near-death experiences had become popular knowledge it was folklore that your life flashed before your eyes as you died. So it does. The light, almost as if it were a movie projector, now exposed my past to me. Exposed the hidden parts. There was no focus upon my sins that I'd consciously regretted or the accomplishments I'd enjoyed. Instead it framed all the scenes of cruelties, large and small, that I'd committed without being aware I'd committed them. There was the time, for instance, I'd adamantly refused to allow our daughter to have her ears pierced, not even bothering to consider the possibility I was making a total unnecessary mountain out of a perfectly benign molehill. It also framed a number of rather decent things I'd done unwittingly, as for the nurse in the emergency room who somehow received great solace once from an offhand remark I'd inadvertently made. The experience was profoundly paradoxical. On the one hand, I was horrified by what a careless and often callous human being I'd been. On the other, the sense of acceptance went on unabated, and I knew I was somehow respected despite it all.

I have no idea how long this life review lasted. I suppose it might have taken but a few seconds. It might also have taken a few years. I know only that a moment came when it was over, and the light was welcoming me to respond.

I blurted out my question. "Are you God?"

The light made no answer and gave me to understand

there would be none. Still, it accepted me. "I don't have to go back, do I?" I asked.

The light exploded with gaiety. "Of course not," it told me with such joyful mirth I knew for certain that not only was there an afterlife but that I'd been admitted to it.

Except at the very next instant I completely blacked out.

CHAPTER

2

W hen I came to I was lying on a sort of bed in a small green room. The room, only about four feet wide and eight feet long, had no windows yet was suffused with light, so the green was the green of young leaves in springtime. There was no lamp. There was no furniture at all. My bed, in fact, was but a green ledge protruding from the wall. There were two smaller such protuberances that I imagined might serve as chairs. Otherwise nothing. No sheets, blankets, drawers, or decorations. It was more of a cubicle or cubbyhole than a room, yet the green and the light made it not unpleasant.

Curious, I pushed my hand against the wall to ascertain what kind of substance it was made of. I felt nothing. For a moment, I thought my hand had gone right through the wall. Expecting to see that was the case, I looked down and saw nothing except the wall. No hand. No shoulder. I glanced down at my feet. No feet either. And no legs, thighs, or torso. It dawned on me then that I had no body.

Mentally I kicked myself for being so slow for coming to the realization. Naturally I had no body. I was dead, wasn't I? I'd left my body back on my bed being wept over by our children.

But then thoughts, questions, answers, and more questions came tumbling one upon another with a rapidity that verged on incoherency.

Mentally I'd kicked myself. What a metaphor! I wouldn't be kicking myself any longer, would I? I had no foot to kick myself with. The notion of kicking myself had been a major part of my thinking for seventy-three years. How would I think now? How many of our mental metaphors presuppose the condition of having a body? Or proverbs? A bird in the hand is worth two in the bush . . . only now I didn't have a hand. All that glitters is not gold. But I no longer had eyes to see anything glitter.

Or did I? I could see the room, its green almost glittering with freshness. But how? If I didn't have a body, I didn't have eyes. Instinctively I reached up to feel for my eyes, yet there was no hand to feel them with. I didn't even know whether I had eyes or not.

Annoyed, I looked around for a mirror. There wasn't one. "What kind of hotel room is this?" I wondered angrily. "They don't even have a mirror!" Then I laughed at myself. I had no reason to believe it was a hotel room. Or that it should have a mirror when I didn't have a body. But my laughter felt hollow, I was so discomfited. And if it wasn't a hotel room, what the hell kind of room was it? I had no idea.

I looked at the room more closely, and all I observed was what wasn't there. There was no toilet, no bathroom. Maybe there was a toilet out in the hall. But how would I get out into the hall? I looked and there was no door. It brilliantly occurred to me that I might not need a toilet at all since I wouldn't need to go to the bathroom if I had no body. What would life be like without having to go to the bathroom? Again I laughed, but again it was hollow. I was beginning to panic.

There was no door. How would I get out of this room? Or back in? Was I stuck here without having to ever go to the bathroom? Was this my cell for eternity? And what in God's name was eternity? For that matter, I didn't even know how long I'd been here already. Minutes? Hours? Days? Weeks? Months? Years? Eons?

There was only one thing I could grab hold of. I was conscious. I was thinking—not well it seemed, but still thinking. Which meant I was alive, didn't it? *Cogito, ergo sum*—"I think, therefore I am." Good old Descartes. Maybe he didn't know it, but he proved the existence of an afterlife . . . at least for me, at least for himself when he got here. Assuming he got here. Did Descartes awaken after death in a little green room to find himself conscious, I wondered, and therefore certain of his existence?

Yes, I was conscious. I was cogitating. But how? If I had no body, I had no brain. How does one think without a brain? Instinctively, again, I reached up for my forehead, and again I felt nothing since I had no hand to feel with. Did that mean I had no head or just no hand? Maybe I was a disembodied head floating around the room. Damn, why were there no mirrors?

Floating around the room . . . was that just another bodily metaphor or could I float? Could I change my position, my vantage point? I imagined myself sitting on the protuberance at the other end of the room looking back at my bed, my pallet. It worked. My vantage point instantly changed. Or had it really? Imagination was not the same as reality. Was I really sitting here looking back at my bed, or was I simply imagining it? I'd been so sure I existed, that I'd made it to the afterlife, but it suddenly occurred to me that perhaps I was just imagining that I existed. For that matter, maybe I hadn't even existed in a past life. Maybe my whole past life, and my death and my being welcomed by the light, had been nothing more than my imagination.

What is reality? What in God's name is reality?

Frightened, I moved back to my bed. It seemed more secure. I leaned back, or at least imagined that I laid an imaginary body back, and tried to think. I felt a little more calm. Damn it, everything wasn't imagination! I hadn't imagined this room. I'd imagined an afterlife before. But never the specifics, and never in my wildest imagination had I thought I'd end up closeted in a little green room. At least not consciously. Was there such a thing as unconscious imagination? Of course. I was a psychiatrist—or had been once upon a time—and knew full well about the wildness of dreams and how they seemed more vivid than the reality of waking. Which just gave me another question: was this all a dream of a sort? And reminded me of the old Zen Buddhist conundrum: "Last night I dreamed I was a butterfly . . . or am I a butterfly today dreaming that I'm a man?"

At this point I was faced with another dilemma. I seemed to be able to imagine myself moving around this little green room. I'd also been worried I might be stuck in it for eternity. Was there a possibility I could imagine myself out of it? I tried to imagine what could be outside, the other side of the walls, and I drew a blank. The fact of the matter was I didn't have the foggiest idea what existed on the other side. Consciously I had no reference point. I supposed I could imagine anything I wanted to. But what happened if I found myself on the other side of the wall and it wasn't anything like what I imagined—the reality might be something horrible. Ultimately I'd been willing to die because, at seventy-three, I'd been tired to death of living. But I was not yet tired of my little green room and not about to take another leap into the unknown right after the first. I was not ready for another death right away.

If only somebody could tell me what lay on the other side! I needed at least that much of a reference point. I needed a teacher, a guide. I desperately needed someone who knew the rules of this place. All my life I'd dimly acknowledged that I needed other people. Over the last two decades that knowledge had become ever more clear. Still, it had been an intellectual sort of thing. Now, for the first time, I realized there was no way I could possibly know what was real without the context of a human society. I recalled the infants who'd been raised without meaningful human contact. They died. Or else they became insane. Alone forever I'd go insane. Without other human beings, no matter how different from me, I was purely lost. And terrified.

"Oh, God," I prayed. "Please help me. Please let there be someone. Please send me somebody."

CHAPTER

3

I mmediately there was a knock on the door. Not stopping to think that there was no door, I cried out, "Come in."

Before I could metaphorically blink, a man and a woman materialized, sitting on the "chairs" that faced my bed. They both appeared to be in their mid forties. The woman, her shoulder-length brown hair neatly coiffed, wore a white blouse and loose, unrevealing black slacks. The man's blond hair was so precise it might have been a toupee. A light blue polo shirt covered the beginnings of a paunch underneath the waist of his beige pants. "Hi," he said. "I'm Sam."

"And I'm Norma," his partner announced.

"I'm Daniel," I responded as if we'd just been introduced on the porch of some beach club. Struck by the inanity of it, however, I added, "I'm glad to see you. I was just feeling a bit lost."

"Of course you were," Norma said with motherly solicitude. "That's why we're here. We've been waiting for you."

"You were expecting me?" I wondered whether they might be the managers of this "club."

Sam nodded. "We're your Greeters. They assigned us to you as soon as you left your body. But we waited for you to have a sleep and a little time to start getting adjusted." He seemed to emphasized the word "start."

I looked at them closely, struck by two things. One was that they both seemed to flicker slightly. The other was their mutual quality of subdued prissiness as if they might be a pair of evangelizing Mormons or Jehovah's Witnesses at my door. I was instinctively prepared to go for their theological jugulars. "You talked about my leaving my body," I commented, "yet you seem to have bodies."

"Seem is the right word," Sam acknowledged. "We don't really, but we can project them when we need to."

"Like now," Norma continued. "If we'd come to you disembodied, our greeting would probably seem to you at this point just like one of your own thoughts, and that would make you feel even more confused. Shall we show him, Sam?"

"Sure," Sam said, and instantly vanished. As did Norma. Yet they were still present as two vague balls of light, and Sam continued speaking. "Anyway, we've come to greet you. People need real people to greet them. Seeing is believing, so to speak."

This last statement he somehow seemed to find amusing. But I couldn't deny the correctness of it. Looking through their ephemeral lights at their empty chairs, it was as if his voice was echoing in my head. Starting to feel disoriented again, I capitulated immediately, while trying not to sound too plaintive. "I'd just as soon you came back."

Norma and Sam reappeared, sitting across from me. Did I imagine a slight sense of self-satisfaction in their posture? Regardless, I was glad to see them again. And to ask the obvious question: "Can you see me?"

"Yes, quite clearly—in a manner of speaking," Norma answered.

"Let me try to explain," Sam said. "Although you've left your actual body behind, your soul, and your personality, if you will, are here intact. You're accustomed to project your personality into your body. We can't see the actual body, the dead thing that's probably buried by now, but you're so accustomed to projecting your spirit into your body, like when you smile, you know, or when you frown—you do it unconsciously—that we can see your projection."

It made sense in a way. But I had a million questions. "You both look to me like you're in your forties," I noted. "I hope you don't mind me asking, but did you both die in middle age?"

"You can ask anything you want," Sam said. "No, I died of a heart attack on the golf course on my sixty-sixth birthday. What a birthday present! How 'bout you, Norma?"

"I died in a nursing home when I was eighty-seven. That was a *real* present. But we were both middle-aged sorts of people, I guess," she continued.

They'd told me I could ask anything I wanted. "Were the two of you married back when you were alive?"

"We *are* alive," Sam emphasized. "You mean were we married when we were in our bodies back on earth? No. We met here at the training for Greeters. They decided we'd make a good pair, and we do, don't we, Norma?" The question was rhetorical. He continued. "We Greeters always work

19

in pairs, usually male and female. But that's just when we're greeting. It's not a marriage. Mostly, we're separate."

A part of me wanted to stay with this line of questioning. Did Norma have a husband back on earth, I wondered? Sam a wife? They'd struck me like Mormons for a moment. Were they still married here to their earthly spouses, as Mormons believed? Here in heaven? If this was heaven, that is. I had an investment in the matter. What might it mean for Mary Martha and me? But I had even more immediate questions. The first was embarrassingly self-centered. "What do I look like to you?" I asked. "Do I look middle-aged?"

Norma smiled. "That's an interesting question," she responded. "You're kind of funny that way. One moment you look to me like an old man. A healthy old man, but very old and very wise. The next moment you look like a boy. Maybe eight years old, filled with energy and exuberance, but maybe not so wise. Maybe not to be trusted. Oh, I don't mean you look like a bad boy. A nice boy, but a boy with mischief, a boy who could get into trouble not because he's mean, but simply because he's so young he doesn't know his limits yet. But the next moment you seem like an old man again. It's strange. Is that the way you see him, Sam?"

"Yes, it's like he vibrates back and forth." Sam nodded in agreement. "We've not seen a soul, a projection, like yours before. But then we haven't been Greeters all that long."

Their appraisal rang true. It was not the first time I'd heard it. An intuitive friend who was a film director once came to listen to me lecture in my middle age. Afterward, she told me how she'd noticed the same vibration between extremes of youth and age. "It was a bit disconcerting," she'd said. "At times I had trouble concentrating on what you were saying

I was so busy watching you vibrate back and forth." And it went further than that. The summer I was sixteen I worked on a farm owned by an elderly lawyer, Mr. Markett. He and I did not get along well together. Which was probably my fault because I could remember Mr. Markett calling me into his study one summer evening and explaining. "I have a great deal of trouble relating to you, Daniel. One day I think you're just about the most immature kid I've ever seen and the next you do or say something that makes me wonder if you're not older and wiser than I am myself."

So Norma and Sam's perceptions were accurate. They weren't blind; to the contrary, their "sight" was remarkably penetrating. But how? "How can you see me so clearly," I asked, "when you don't have eyes? And me see you—or your projections—when I presumably don't have them either?"

"I don't know," Sam said.

I was aghast. "You don't know?"

"Nope. Maybe in some way we can project our eyes just like we can project our bodies, but I don't really know."

I pressed forward. "For a moment a while back you abolished your bodies . . . your projections. I couldn't see you. I couldn't see your eyes—just your lights. Could you still see me back then?"

"Yes."

"But how if you didn't even have projected eyes to see with?"

"As I said, I don't know," Sam answered patiently. "Maybe it's sort of like ESP."

Ah, yes, good old extrasensory perception. Which begged the question. Or did it? The million-dollar question. Might they have the million-dollar answer? I asked. "And how does ESP work?"

"We don't know," Norma replied.

I was disappointed, frustrated. "And I suppose you'd give the same answer about unexplainable ESP to the question of how you can hear me without ears? Or me hear you?"

"Yup," Sam nodded.

"And how we can speak to each other without tongues?"

"Yup."

My frustration was on the verge of turning into annoyance. "Does anyone know? Is there anyone who knows how this sort of ESP works?"

"We don't know that either," Norma said.

"Have you asked? Have you looked for someone who knows?"

"No."

"Dammit, aren't you curious?"

"No."

I felt as if I was almost screaming at them. "How can you not be curious?"

"Look, Daniel, we're not like you," Sam said calmly but with great deliberateness. "You didn't expect to come to an afterlife where everyone was alike, did you? We're just ordinary people. You're a doctor, a scientist, a theologian, a man who's spent most of his life on an intellectual frontier. But I was just the sales manager for a small company in Dayton, Ohio, and never the sort of person who had the need to think about big things."

"And I just the wife of a farmer near Topeka, Kansas," Norma added, "much the same as Sam. I believed in love. I tried to be loving as best I could, and that seemed to take about all the energy I had for pondering."

I felt gently, albeit quite correctly, chastened. I thought I'd spent much of the last half of my life coming to terms with how different I was from others, how different everyone was from each other more or less, and how much we needed those differences. But it looked as if I hadn't come anywhere near to finishing the job. Of course I had no reason to expect everyone to be alike here. Mary Martha and I had loved to travel. That was part of the glue of our marriage. We were explorers, and naturally most of our close friends were explorers too. But we knew perfectly well that we were in a minority, that the average person had no great desire to ever leave Ohio or Kansas, much less the United States. And who was to say that our restless curiosity was somehow superior to their lack of restlessness—they who often had the gift to be simple?

Norma interrupted my reverie. "And we're not Mormons," she said with a hint of a giggle. "I was a Lutheran."

"I wasn't much of anything," Sam chimed in. "A lukewarm Methodist, I guess. I had a relationship with the Lord, but I kept it pretty much to myself."

"So you can also read minds," I commented with a blush.

"Just the minds of those that don't mind being read," Sam explained. "People are free. That's something we'll have to talk about shortly. Those that want their thoughts to stay hidden are free to keep them that way. I guess you're a person who never had much need to keep secrets. In fact you're just about the most transparent person we've ever greeted, wouldn't you say, Norma?"

"I'd say so, Sam."

Again they were right on the mark. I wasn't exactly sure I

liked their ability to read my first impression of them, but I was, in fact, a person who liked to speak my mind whenever I could. I was able to keep secrets, but generally preferred not to. It was simply another way that I was a bit different. They were correct that most people were by nature more secretive than I.

"Okay, I surrender," I smiled. "I'm sorry I misjudged you, not that I really have anything more against Mormons than I do against Lutherans, lukewarm Methodists, or myself. I'm sorry I assumed that you'd be like me and have my same kind of curiosity. I'm sorry I jumped to the conclusion that because you were Greeters you'd have all the answers."

"Apologies accepted," Sam said.

"But I still have questions, whether you can answer them or not."

"Of course you do," Norma said approvingly.

"Shoot," Sam welcomed.

"You said that 'they' had assigned you to greet me, and you implied that 'they' had selected and trained you as Greeters. Who are 'they'?"

"They're sort of like a committee," Sam answered, "only they're much smarter than us."

"You're going to ask whether 'they' are God," Norma jumped in, "and the best we can do is to say 'sort of.' How do we know they're smarter than us? That we know to obey?"

"When you hear God, you know," Sam continued, filling in the answers, "just as you know the light you entered when you left your body was not only welcoming but benign. You didn't need to question it."

"You'll also wonder when you yourself might hear from

this committee. Or meet it. Or see it. Or see God," Norma fed in. "And again we're going to have to say, 'We don't know.' Except that it will happen when you're ready for it. If you're ready for it, and I expect he will be, don't you, Sam?"

"Expect so," Sam agreed. "Daniel seems pretty open and growing to me."

I became aware that Norma and Sam were moving very fast, answering my questions before I asked them. It was as if they were continually reading my mind now—and maybe I was even reading theirs—more than as if we were having a normal "down to earth" conversation. I was also aware, with no small amount of chagrin, that this speed was occurring precisely because I had allowed it, because I had surrendered to the two of them on a certain level. I was no longer getting in the way. And rather than feeling almost overwhelmed as I had in our earlier dialogue, I was actually grateful for the extraordinary efficiency of this new level of communication.

Still, I had questions. Particularly the big one. "Is this heaven, hell, or purgatory?" I demanded.

"Take your pick," Norma shot back.

Sam went a little slower on my behalf. "I said we'd be getting back to the subject of freedom," he reminded me. "The governing law of the afterlife is what we call the Principle of Freedom. There is absolutely nothing that's coercive here. Souls are free to respond to this place or level of existence in any way they choose. Some choose it to be hell, some purgatory, and some heaven. You'll be wondering how and why they make this choice. Why would anyone choose hell, for instance? I could give you an intellectual explanation, but I think it will mean more when you find out for yourself.

Which you will. And I don't think he needs to worry about it being hell for himself, does he, Norma?"

"No, he doesn't," Norma pronounced definitively. "He's not the sort."

"It doesn't seem like hell to me," I acknowledged, "but it also doesn't feel like heaven. So I guess it must be purgatory."

"Ah, purgatory," Sam sighed. "It sounds like a vicious laxative, designed to bend a man double with pain. It *is* a cleansing. But those old physicians on earth who used such painful purgatives were trying to heal, only they didn't know much about how. This is a gentle place. A healing place if you want to be healed. And if one wants to be healed it's sometimes hard to tell the difference between heaven and purgatory. Besides, everyone who comes here, no matter how good or holy they are, needs a period of adjustment. That's our job as Greeters: to do the best we can to help newcomers with the Adjustment."

Sam hadn't said *my* adjustment. He'd said *the* Adjustment, as if it were something very major. I suddenly had a vision of a horde of mechanics applying wrenches to me, adjusting me here and there, this way and that. I began to feel anxious again. "What's the Adjustment?"

"Yes, it is a big thing," Sam answered, reading my thoughts again, "but it's nothing mechanical; it's nothing that's done to you. It's just an inevitable period required to get used to a new state of being. You've already begun it. Almost as soon as you awoke you were feeling disoriented, even a bit frightened, because you didn't have a body. It takes some getting used to, not having a body."

"That's for sure," I agreed.

"But it's much bigger than just that," Norma continued. "The body is matter, and there's no matter here; there's no space. And because there's no space, there's no time. Remember how much adjusting the astronauts had to do to get used to weightlessness in outer space? Some of that was physical. They still had bodies, and those bodies had to adjust. But much of it was psychological, and they still had their bodies and the material of their spaceships and their clocks ticking away. If it took some adjusting just to get used to weightlessness, think of what it takes to get used to bodilessness, spacelessness, and timelessness!"

I was aghast. "There's no time here?"

"Not in the ordinary sense," Norma went on. "You may recall Sam saying that your body's probably been buried by now. But we don't know that. We don't know whether your body died an hour ago, a day ago, a week ago, or a year ago. How long do you think you were in the Light? You don't have the foggiest idea, do you? Or how long you slept afterward? We don't know how long we've even been having this conversation. Maybe it's just been a second or two, the way so many things can seem to happen in the space of a short dream. There are no clocks, you see."

Norma smiled at me. "There is some kind of time here. We refer to it as God's time. And immediately you're going to want to ask us, 'How does God's time work?' and we're going to tell you again that we don't know. It's God's time, not ours. Well, in a sense, it's our time too in that we participate in it. Still, we don't begin to understand it. And, no, we haven't tried. Perhaps with your curiosity you'll try to figure it out. Yet I'm not at all sure you'll succeed. As I said, it's God's time."

I was not annoyed at their lack of curiosity as I'd been before. They'd not been giving me all the answers I wanted, but it was amazing how many they were giving me now that I'd stopped demanding them. Still, the scientist in me rebelled slightly. "What about this room?" I asked. "You say there's no space, yet here we're sitting in this little green room. It's a space. I'm sitting on a bed. You're sitting on something like chairs. There are walls. Aren't they all of some material or another?"

Sam grinned. "Nope."

I bit my metaphorical tongue. "Go on," I urged.

"The room's no more material than the bodies we're projecting. In part it's only a projection of yours."

"I didn't imagine it," I protested. "Never on earth did I see or dream of a room like this. It's not my projection. I had no part in its creation."

"What's your favorite color?" Sam asked with seeming innocence.

"Green," I admitted ruefully.

"You're right that it's not solely your creation," Sam said consolingly. "They have also created it. It's their projection too."

"They?"

"Yes, sort of like the committee that selected and trained us as Greeters. Only it's a different committee. Or else it's God. We don't really know. God and committees seem to be all mixed up here. And if you ask how they do it, once again we're going to have to tell you that we don't know."

I tried to put together the few pieces that I did have. "So what you're telling me is that this room isn't real in a materialistic sense but it does exist as a kind of combined thought form—an imaginary co-creation of them and me? Or God and me."

"Yup."

"But why? Why would they go to all the trouble?"

"I doubt it's all that much trouble for them," Sam answered, "but they do it because you need a place. I mean, you've got enough trouble adjusting without a place. We all do. Everyone's given a place for the duration of the Adjustment."

Yes, indeed, I needed a place. Although Mary Martha and I had been great travelers and adventurers of a sort, we had always needed a snug hotel at the end of a day's journey. So much so we never traveled without reservations during our later years. We used to joke about it. Our nesting instinct, we called it. I felt a wave of gratitude. "So they've prepared a place for me," I noted.

"Yup," Sam replied as if it was the most natural thing in the world. Then he went on. "Adjustment to the loss of body, space, and time is just part of it, and part of why we need a place. The bigger adjustment comes more gradually. It's the adjustment to freedom."

"To freedom?" I echoed.

"Yup. In a sense it's related. You're not bound by your body anymore, so you can go wherever you want whenever you want. But it goes much deeper. Remember when you asked whether this was hell, heaven, or purgatory, Norma and I told you you could take your pick and how souls are free to choose either way. That kind of freedom can be frightening."

"We suggest you take it easy at first," Norma interjected. "It's perfectly safe. As Sam said, it's a gentle place. But it'll be full of surprises for you for a good while. For instance, you were wondering what's outside this room. You're perfectly free to leave it anytime you want—and come back here anytime you want—but you won't know what it'll look like until you do leave and you'll have no idea whom you might meet. Not that you'll be in any danger. It's just that you'll need to be prepared for surprises, and that may take some thinking."

"Even prayer," Sam added.

"You mean I'll be meeting other souls," I inquired, "kind of like we're meeting now?"

"Kind of," Sam responded, "but only kind of. It'll be different each time. And I already hear you asking whether you can meet particular souls such as your wife or other people who've passed on. The answer is yes . . . but only if they want to meet you. Remember the Principle of Freedom applies here. Let's take your wife. That's close to home. You might want to see her again, but she might not want to see you. That would be a shocker, wouldn't it?"

"And then you couldn't see her no matter how much you wanted to or how upset her rejection might make you," Norma followed up. "Furthermore, even if she did want to see you, she might be very different from what you expected. People change, you know. This may be God's time, but its still time, so things change. What would be the point otherwise?"

Although much earlier I'd felt annoyed, now for the first time in our conversation I felt on overload. The issues surrounding the question of whether I wanted to meet certain people, Mary Martha, in particular, and whether they would want to meet me . . . and how they might have changed . . . or I might have changed myself . . . were so profound I couldn't digest them. Sam and Norma were right—it would take time and prayer. I jumped to a different aspect of freedom. "You said I'm free to go anywhere, anytime. Can I go to other planets and galaxies?" I wanted to know. "Can I go back to earth? Can I see people on earth, like old friends still there or my children? Can I go back in time? Can I go forward in time?" My questions tumbled forth.

"The answer to all of them is yes," Sam replied. "But just as the Principle of Freedom holds true here, the Law of Non-Interference also prevails. No matter how much we might love them—or hate them—we are not supposed to interfere with other people or places. I don't mean to imply that this law is never broken. Occasionally it is broken by an individual soul, almost invariably for ill. Occasionally by a committee for benefit. But should you even begin to consider breaking it, we urge you—we beg you—to call us back for a consultation first."

"While here freedom prevails," Norma added, "please remember that other places and people may not be so free. They may not be able to stop you from interfering. That's why if you did interfere it would probably be a violation of them."

It made perfect sense. I understood it on an intellectual level, but I was starting to feel dazed. At that point I, or my projected body, did something I hadn't anticipated. I yawned.

"Oh, you're getting tired, poor dear," Norma clucked.

"Well of course he is," Sam announced. "He's had a lot to take in, hasn't he? It's time we left him to get some sleep."

I was tired, but I snapped awake at this. "Sleep?" I asked. "Why should I need to sleep when I don't have a body?"

"Sleep's not primarily a matter of the body," Sam explained. "It's mostly a matter of the soul. Souls get tired, you know. Think about when you were back on earth, about some time when you were terribly fatigued. Was it really your body that was so fatigued, or was it your soul?"

There were many such times, and Sam was right. " 'I'm tired to the bone,' we used to say," I commented. "But you're correct. Usually my bones weren't actually aching; it was just someplace deep inside of me. I guess it was my soul."

"Exactly!" Norma exclaimed. "So you went to sleep right after you'd been with the Light, didn't you? Of course you did. Then you had even more to take in than now. Still, this has been rich, hasn't it, Sam?"

"Yup. A lot to digest, as they say. Just one thing more. Call us whenever you need. As you know by now, we can't answer all your questions, but maybe you'll have some others we can help with."

"Then again, maybe he won't," Norma rebutted Sam gently. "He doesn't have to call us back. This is a place of freedom. Daniel's not obliged to call us back. He can call whomever he wants whenever he wants. But we'll come if you call."

"How? How do I call?"

"Just the way you did before we came in," Norma informed me. "You were petitioning for someone to come. It was us because we were waiting for you. Next time it will be us if you specifically ask for us. It'll be someone else if you specifically petition for someone else."

The word "petition" caught my attention. Petitionary prayer. "I wasn't just petitioning for someone to come," I noted. "I was *praying* for someone to come. I was desperate."

"Desperation tends to make for good prayer, doesn't it," Norma remarked with a smile. And at that both she and Sam vanished. They were just gone. Not light forms anymore, but gone, and I was all alone again in my little green room.

CHAPTER

4

I *was* tired. I was also too chagrined for the moment to rest. Perhaps it was no big matter for them, but in their "ordinariness" I felt I had not treated Norma and Sam with the respect they deserved. It was time to wrestle once again, here, now, in the afterlife as back on earth, with my "Daniel complex."

I'd been christened Daniel Turpin, named after a great-great-grandfather I'd obviously never met. He was apparently a man of so little note my family could tell me nothing about him. He was a blank. But being his namesake came to often feel like a kind of curse that had been laid upon me.

The curse began in Sunday school when I first heard that little vignette about Daniel being thrown into the lions' den. I believe I was around eight years old. It didn't help that afterwards the other children chanted at me, "Daniel, Daniel Turpin, they're going to throw you into the lions' den." But I suspect that simply hearing the story was enough, and for the rest of my life I felt as if the lions' den, or some equivalent, was right around the corner. All I had to do was make one significant misstep! I was, to put it mildly, a relatively anxious man.

Psychoanalysis when I reached the age of thirty was of some assistance. My analyst didn't eat me. Despite the fact I thoroughly bared my soul to him, he seemed not to consider me a suitable candidate for lion fodder. Much as this reassurance was healing—my blood pressure came down—I remained however an anxious creature. No matter that the lions didn't eat Daniel, I knew that they had soon dramatically munched upon his enemies. And while I always had friends, I was also always somebody's enemy.

Now I realized my anxiety had followed me into the afterlife. I'd been virtually rude to Sam and Norma in my eagerness—almost insistence—to get answers. Why? Why couldn't I have been more properly laid back? I suspected that my thirst for knowledge here as well as back on earth was partly motivated by a fear that if I didn't have all the answers right away I might make one of those missteps that would end me up with the lions.

There was more than just anxiety to my Daniel complex. Oddly enough, it wasn't until age sixty that I actually read the Book of Daniel in the Old Testament, and I was thunderstruck by some of the similarities between the mythical Daniel and myself.

The book begins with Daniel being in exile. In his case the exile was with other Jews from Jerusalem in Babylon as captives of King Nebuchadnezzar. Although I myself had never been physically exiled, the concept was a poignant one for me. For reasons I could never explain, I'd lived my entire adult life with a muted yet profound sense that the earth was not my true home. My life had been full of joys, but always tinged with a yearning for some Jerusalem that existed I knew not where. Regardless of reality, I'd felt myself to be an exiled being of a sort.

Also at the beginning of the story the mythical Daniel had been selected by the king as one of the brightest and the best, so to speak. And so had I, examination by examination, diploma by diploma. Why? Norma and Sam had referred to themselves as ordinary people, unlike me. My being extra-ordinary, supposedly one of the brightest and the best, had never seemed to me like an achievement. Rather it had al-ways struck me as an inexplicable bit of luck . . . and occa-sionally a curse. I'd spent a great deal of time off and on won-dering, "Why me?" and not infrequently had wished I could be ordinary.

Shortly the Daniel of the Book began to gain a consider-able reputation as an interpreter of dreams. He was a kind of Old Testament psychiatrist. I too had become a psychia-trist, and though not infallible like him, I did have a certain talent for dream interpretation myself. By virtue of his tal-ents, Daniel had been made a high-ranking administrator. I also had become a psychiatric administrator for a while but hardly one of great rank.

After his bout with the lions, Daniel seemed to make an-other career change, not so much interpreting the dreams of others as pronouncing his own visions. In a sense that was what happened to me. In midlife I had gradually moved from the role of psychiatrist to the role of author and public speaker. Never did I consider myself a prophet like the bib-lical Daniel, but it might be said that I had become something of a theologian and visionary.

Of course none of this happened because I was trying to imitate my biblical namesake since I only read about him after the fact. Yet it did seem as if by some quirk of fate I'd been following in his footsteps. Not that we had similar personalities. To the contrary, the Daniel of the Bible apparently had none of my failings. No mention was made of him being unhappy with his exile. He was as calm as I was anxious. The lions' den didn't seem to worry him in the least. Indeed, he was threatened with it if he didn't stop praying to his God for just a few days, yet he deliberately continued to pray. Would I have been so faithful to God? I doubted it. Relative to most people, I did pray quite a lot, but the biblical Daniel was *always* on his knees and possessed a degree of trust in God as well as a depth of courage I clearly lacked.

So yet another part of my Daniel complex was a certain haunting sense of my own personal inadequacy relative to his perfection. But it wasn't something that weighed on me too heavily. I referred to him as "the mythical Daniel," and so he was. The Book of Daniel describes him as serving or confronting an almost endless succession of kings, and Bible scholars are generally agreed that he was a composite figure to represent a whole number of different Jewish leaders during the period of exile. Besides, he was just too good to be true. He never wondered, "Why me, Lord?" I found it hard to empathize with him. Year after year the bastard was never once fainthearted, much less plain tired. In fact, he never even seemed to sleep.

It was at this point, having worked myself through the paces of my Daniel complex and habitual guilt, that I began to relax. In fact, I started to feel as relieved as I'd ever felt before in my life. It had to do with the business of sleeping.

Sleep is one of the many ways we are all so different. Back on earth some people seemed to get along fine on five or six hours of sleep a night. Not me. I needed nine, and I felt horrible if I didn't get it. Oh, I could get by on seven for a couple of nights running, but then it was like I would die if I didn't catch up. Mary Martha was a different type. She too needed nine hours, but she never felt awful with less, the way I did when I was deprived. She'd just get more and more wound up without knowing why, and often it was as if I'd practically have to order her to bed like a child. She never worried about not getting enough sleep; me, I was continually haunted by the prospect. That was why I was so relieved—that and the ghastly Sufi story which had haunted me for years.

It was a story about a good Muslim. He was considerate of his wife and kind to his children. He'd been successful at commerce but gave most of his money away to the poor. He'd made his pilgrimage to Mecca and faithfully attended public prayers every Friday at the mosque. He served conscientiously on many charitable boards and committees in his city. If he had any fault or limitation, any at all, it was that he liked his sleep.

Well, one day he expired, as we all must, and found himself outside the proverbial pearly gates being greeted by St. Peter (or the Muslim equivalent). St. Peter greeted him so warmly the man was emboldened to ask, "Are these really the Gates of Heaven?" And added, because he was also a humble man, "Have I really lived a good enough life to be admitted to Heaven?"

"Of course," St. Peter answered. "You've led an exemplary life. Of course a man of your caliber will be admitted to Heaven. But there is one slight problem. The Gates of Heaven open only once every five hundred years. So just have a seat under that tree over there, and as soon as they open you can walk right in. But stay alert because the Gates aren't open for very long."

The man did as instructed and waited under the tree. Naturally, after a while he began to grow tired, then very, very tired. He kept blinking for what seemed like an eternity. Finally, he decided it wouldn't hurt if he closed his eyes for just a minute or two. He did so and dozed off. Then he was awoken from his brief slumber by a loud CLANG—the sound of the Gates of Heaven clanging shut.

I knew it was a story to teach the virtues of consciousness—something I myself had preached in my books. But I had never preached it so harshly. Even at the final conclusion of the Book of Daniel God tells Daniel that he can rest.

Sam and Norma had told me this was a gentle place. And that sleep was for the soul. It was still not precisely clear that I was within the Gates of Heaven, but it seemed as if I might be. Certainly it seemed I could allow myself to drift off. And so I did.

CHAPTER

5

T his time when I awoke it was more like it had been back on earth. There was some sort of dreaming. As always for me, it was pleasant, and I tried to cling to my dreams, waging the usual struggle to keep them from slipping away, to resist ordinary consciousness. As always, I lost. The moment came when I reluctantly concluded, "I might as well get up and face the morning."

Of course it was unnecessary that I get up in a bodily sense, and I had no idea whether it was morning, afternoon, or evening. But I was awake in my little green room. Its glittering light that came from God-knows-where made it seem like morning. Customarily I wondered, "What do I have to do today?"

The answer was a shock. Nothing. I didn't *have* to do anything.

My first feeling was one of loss. I would miss putting on my slippers and going downstairs to the kitchen . . . miss squeezing myself a glass of fresh orange juice and feeding the cats ... miss making a cup of coffee and taking it back to bed with me for my first cigarette of the day.

But there were other things I definitely would not miss. Flossing my teeth, for instance. My back exercises. Thank God. I would never *have* to do back exercises again.

Would I miss smoking? I hadn't yet. There'd not been any of that sensation of rats gnawing at the insides of my rib cage. But then I had no rib cage, no lungs, and no brain to send me messages that its chemicals were getting desperate. I rather liked the idea. Perhaps liberation from my body would mean liberation from my addictions. Liberty!

Yet how would I mark the time? T.S. Eliot's insipid anti-hero, Prufrock, confided, "I have measured out my life with coffee spoons." Well, I'd measured out mine with cigarettes at the rate of just about one each waking hour, marking out my moments of stress and boredom. What now? Yes, my time was completely free. It was also empty.

Sam and Norma had warned me that the greater part of the Adjustment would be in dealing with freedom. I hoped I was better prepared than most. On earth I had extolled the spiritual virtues of "emptiness." I'd taught thousands of people the ways they could empty themselves of preconceptions and expectations, their prejudices and judgmentalism—how they could free themselves from mental rigidity and destructive, habitual ways of relating with each other. I taught them silence and contemplation. I taught them emptiness. And I had practiced what I preached. So I was not frightened as I'd first been yesterday—if it was yesterday. I was not frightened of "the emptiness of not knowing," of not even knowing whether it was morning or night; yesterday, today, or tomorrow; the freedom of not knowing what I would do or how I would fill my time. But I was also deeply familiar with how terrifying the adjustment to such emptiness and freedom could be for most people. And I was glad for myself that I at least had my little green room to cling to as a center in the void.

Still, I needed to begin thinking about liberating myself from the confines of this little room. Temporarily, anyway. As I had taught, the purpose of emptying one's mind was not to ultimately have an empty mind: it was to make space for the new, the unexpected. And the reason for my empty time now wasn't to do nothing: it was to be free to have new experiences. "They" had prepared this room for me so that I could have a haven in the void of freedom, an anchor against aimlessness. Instinctively, however, I knew that I had to leave here to learn anything more.

So I had an adventure ahead of me. An adventure is going into the unknown. Again, I think the prospect was perhaps easier for me than other souls. I flashed back to my psychoanalysis forty-three years before. Although my analyst had a couch in his office, we began our work together by sitting kitty-corner from each other. From time to time I would eye the couch. One morning, after twenty sessions, I remarked, "I think I'd like to take the couch."

"Why?" Dr. Akeley inquired.

A simple question, yet for a few minutes I was lost. As a budding psychoanalyst myself, I knew all the reasons therapists might ask their patients to take the couch. None of them applied in this instance. I was as comfortable as anyone can be in analysis. Our work was proceeding well. Finally, I answered, almost reluctantly, the truth seemed so inane. "Because it's there," I said. "Maybe it sounds silly, but

I'd simply like to have the experience of what it's like to be a patient on the couch. I certainly wouldn't want to leave here without ever having had that experience."

A few sessions later he let me take the couch.

"Because it's there," I'd said. So too had Sir Edmund Hillary answered when asked why he wanted to climb Mt. Everest. I was never physically adventurous like Sir Edmund, but that moment had first put me in touch with the fact that on an intellectual level I did indeed have an adventurous streak in me.

So it was time I left my little green room to discover whatever was out there. Not that I wasn't a bit frightened. It was the unknown. Still, I had to know. But how to get out? I'd learned I could float around my room merely by imagining myself at different places in it. Could I simply imagine myself a few feet past the other side of the wall? I tried it.

Instantly I was in a gray corridor. It was not as well lit as my room, nor as pleasant. Empty of decoration or any sign of use, it felt gloomy and impersonal. It curved gently so I could see only a few hundred feet in either direction. I found myself wishing it was like a hotel corridor with doors and numbers, maybe a tray of discarded food against the wall, maybe some dropped candy-wrapping on the floor—anything to even slightly relieve its dreadful anonymity. But there was nothing. Almost frantically I wished myself back in my little green room.

And so I was. "No sooner said than done," I thought to myself, glad at my maneuverability and glad for the better light and color. Nonetheless, I was discomfited. The gray anonymity of the corridor made me aware for the first time of the anonymity of my own little room. It was better than no place, which is what the corridor had felt like, but at least they could have hung a picture, put down a carpet with some semblance of design. They—they, the Committee, the gods or God—had prepared a place for me, yes, but whereas before my sleep I'd appreciated their graciousness, now I was annoyed. They hadn't seemed to have exerted themselves all that much. It was all so utterly *functional*. Just a space and nothing more.

But what to do now? The corridor was hardly welcoming, yet there'd be no point to only stay in the room. At least I might explore the corridor a bit. Carefully. Maybe there'd be something to learn. A thought occurred to me. I wasn't sure I'd be so willing to explore the corridor if my room were less functional and more interesting. Might it be that they had deliberately made my space uninteresting in order to encourage me to leave it and go exploring? That they wanted me to be adventurous? That it was all designed to facilitate the Adjustment?

Encouraged either by design or oversight, I wished myself out into the corridor again. It was as before. Since there was no door or number, I was anxious that there'd be no way to locate my room if I went exploring too far. I'd best measure my steps. A lions' den might await if I failed to do so. But then I had no steps to measure. And should I go right or left? What I decided was to wish myself to the right but only that distance I could see—about a hundred feet. I did so but then was unsure whether I'd moved at all since the corridor looked just the same.

There was only one way I could think to determine if I'd moved: wish myself to the other side of the wall, not knowing what I'd find. What I found was a room exactly like my own save this one was light blue. It too glittered. It was empty. I could see no one on its pallet. I could sense no presence. Was this because it was waiting for a new occupant? I wondered. Or did it have an occupant who had simply gone out exploring the way I had? Feeling as if I might be violating someone else's space, I thought I'd best quickly leave. Should I retrace my moves—out into the corridor, back down it a hundred feet, then back through the wall? That seemed the safe, human thing to do. But I remembered Norma and Sam telling me that space did not exist here as on earth. Might it be possible to simply wish myself from this room back into my own? It would be more efficient if it worked. But would it work? What if it didn't? It was risky.

At that point I had an experience similar to ones I'd had from time to time during my earthly life. It was as if I heard a "still, small voice" inside me. It said, "Take the risk." I'd learned to identify this voice as the Holy Spirit, what the Quakers called the inner light. I'd also learned to obey it—generally. To obey it always required a small amount of courage. Yet disobeying it had always left me feeling disloyal. I took the risk.

It worked! I was back in my little green room. And with a lot to think about.

I didn't want to jump to conclusions. Still, there were a number of intriguing possibilities. The analogy of a hotel had come to mind several times. I'd angrily wondered why there weren't any mirrors in "this damn hotel." Then just a while ago I'd found myself wishing for trays of uneaten food out in the corridor. But until now they'd been mere analogies. Now I knew there was at least one other room similar to mine, and the long corridor suggested there might be many more. Although without room service trays or mirrors, maybe this was indeed a hotel of sorts designed to house those of us going through the Adjustment.

It also seemed I could go anywhere I wanted in this hotel, or at least back to my own room, whenever I wished simply by wishing it. Could I go anywhere at all? Norma and Sam had suggested so. For the moment, however, I was quite content to stay in the hotel, having thus far ventured no more than a hundred feet from my own room. But to move simply by wishing . . . yes, indeed, it was freedom . . . freedom with a capital *F*, simultaneously frightening and exhilarating.

Finally, it seemed as if the Holy Spirit was operative here just as back on earth. God was with me! I don't know why this struck me with surprise. I was already certain of the existence of an afterlife, and as a theologian I knew that wherever there was life there was God. Why shouldn't I have assumed God's presence here?

So, emboldened by the continued presence of God with me in some form, I wished myself out in the corridor again. To the right or to the left this time? The right had proven satisfactory thus far. Okay, let's go right. I was dimly aware that in thinking "let's" I was thinking "us," including some other being or beings with me. Was it the Committee? Them? God? The gods?

No matter. I wished myself a hundred feet to the right, about to where I'd been before outside of the blue room. Then boldly I "leaped" a hundred feet farther down the corridor. The corridor was still the same, gray, lifeless, unpleasing, but I felt something different. I felt the presence of sadness. Loneliness and unhappiness. The presence seemed to be just on the other side of the wall. Without thinking, I knocked on the wall. Actually, I didn't know how to knock. I did what Norma and Sam must have done when they visited me: I wished or thought a knock.

Immediately it was answered. *"Entrez,"* the response came back.

I entered. This time the room, with the same functional architecture, was pink. Leaning back on its pallet was a hugely fat young woman in a matching pink chiffon dress. It reminded me of a girl's ballet costume only it was much too small, revealing what shouldn't be revealed: gigantically bulging upper arms and thighs and only deep creases to indicate her wrists and ankles. She was wearing pink slippers with clashing purple pompoms. Her hair was blond and set in ringlets like I'd seen before only in daguerreotypes of nineteenth-century brides. She was an incongruous sight. I introduced myself. "I'm Daniel."

"And I am Letitia," she replied in a surprisingly pleasant soprano voice, but with a regal tone that grated on me. "You may, however, refer to me as Tish."

"Are you French?" I inquired, curious about her command of *"Entrez,"* and wondering whether souls here could transcend language.

"No, I am American," she answered, "but you might say that I'm cultured."

My mind was working very fast. As far back as I could remember I had had a prejudice against fat people, men as well as women—not plump or chunky or moderately overweight people, as Mary Martha had been in her later years, but those we physicians called the extremely obese. I suspected that Tish's "body" was merely a projection, but it seemed to be at least a three-hundred-pound one on a woman not much over five feet. And, if that wasn't enough, with her *"Entrez"* and pretense at culture, Tish perfectly fit the stereotype of Miss Piggy of TV fame. Why do stereotypes, reality, and prejudice have to be all so mixed up, I wondered?

My prejudice unfortunately had only been enhanced by my experience as a psychiatrist. I had attempted psychotherapy with half a dozen extremely obese women and men. It had not been successful. All six had a feature in common: a difficulty one way or another in distinguishing between fantasy and reality. Still, that didn't mean that all extremely obese people were that way. I wanted to be fully present for Tish, and to do that I needed to empty myself of both my prejudice and my limited experience.

"I knocked," I said, "because I sensed you might be in some distress."

"Distress? No, I'm not in distress," Tish replied. "Boredom maybe, but distress, no."

"Perhaps that was all I sensed—that you might need some company," I acknowledged. "Do you mind me talking with you for a while?"

Instead of answering, Tish blurted out a question. "What do I look like?"

"A young woman," I responded out of kindness or faint-heartedness. "You look to me to be in your early twenties."

"Yes, yes, but am I beautiful?"

"Well, you're overweight," I stammered. "I know of men who are attracted to heavy women and would find you beautiful."

"Damn and double-damn," Tish exclaimed. She was practically spitting with rage.

"It seems to make you angry," I commented mildly in my old manner as a psychiatrist.

"Of course I'm angry. They promised me a perfect body when I got here, didn't they?"

"They?" I inquired. "Who are they?"

"I don't know. The Bible. The church or something. Some Christians came to talk with me once. They said I'd have a perfect body."

I wasn't sure how to proceed. It was true some Christians talked about a perfect body someday. In fact, the Nicene Creed spoke of the resurrection of the body. But even though I considered myself a Christian, it was one of those relatively few fine points of doctrine I'd never taken seriously. Indeed, my assessment of it even back on earth was that it was a sop the church threw out to people who couldn't imagine any existence at all, any afterlife, without a body. Regardless, Tish had used the phrase, "when I got here." She seemed to know she was here now, and not there. Probably she knew that her old body had died. But that was an assumption. How to test it? "Have you met any people calling themselves the Greeters?" I asked.

Tish said she had.

I couldn't assume her Greeters were the same as mine. "What were their names?" I asked.

"Jonathan and Rebecca."

"And what did they look like?"

"They're pretty and handsome," Tish told me, her envy blatant. "They're in their thirties. Goddamn Yuppies. 'The beautiful people.' "

They didn't sound like Sam and Norma. I had a hunch. "So they looked as if they had 'perfect bodies'?"

"Yes."

"But did they tell you their bodies weren't real? That they were projections? And that your own body now is just a projection?"

"Oh, they keep saying something of the sort."

"But you don't believe them?"

"Well. . . ." Tish was hesitant. "Maybe I do. Maybe I don't."

"Did they show you how they could make their bodies go away?"

"Yes."

"But you're still not sure?"

Tish was emphatic. "Maybe their bodies are projections, but mine isn't. And mine's still fat. You said so yourself."

I wanted to counter that only her projection was still fat, but I held myself in check. Hadn't she just insisted that her body was not a projection? It would be useless to oppose such insistence, I knew. So I switched gears. "Some people told you you'd have a perfect body when you got here," I commented. "It sounds as if your body back on earth must have died."

Tish nodded. She seemed to have no trouble accepting that she was dead in that sense. "How old was it when it died?" I went on.

"I was fifty-four."

"And what did you die from?"

"Obesity, of course." Here again Tish seemed to have no trouble with reality. "Oh, I had high cholesterol. Then I had a heart attack. Then a gallbladder infection, but they had trouble operating. So I got pneumonia. But it was all the complications of obesity. The doctors made that very clear."

"And I bet they tried to make you feel guilty about it," I commented.

Tish seemed uninterested in the matter. I persisted, however, hoping it might build some sort of rapport between us. "They sure tried to make *me* feel guilty," I confided. "I had cancer of the lungs and kept smoking. It was worse because I used to be a physician myself. 'You're a doctor,' they kept saying to me; 'if anyone should know better, you should.' Of course they didn't stop to consider that I might not have been all that keen on living any longer. That my cigarettes were like friends to me. And that maybe my addiction wasn't totally under my own control. It's the same with obesity. Doctors keep thinking it should be a simple thing to diet, even when they know that weight can be hereditary or due to purely biological factors they don't understand yet."

It was, I thought, a pretty speech. Tish yawned.

I tried once more. "You don't seem inclined to regard the 'body' you have as a projection," I said. "I'm trying to understand that, but it's not easy for me because I'm kind of dense. I keep forgetting how different people are. For me, you see, my body was always mainly a nuisance. I always seemed to be getting a head cold or the flu. Sex was wonderful when it was possible—sometimes—but most of the time I was just miserably horny. My back went bad, and as I got old it was nothing but aches and pains. So I'm glad to be rid of the damn thing. But then, as I say, people are different."

"You're right, you don't understand." Tish had become animated now. "You don't know what it's like to be fat. You can see it in everyone's eyes. You can see they think you're ugly. You can see them recoil. Every time. Every waking moment it's all that you think about: 'I'm ugly, ugly, ugly.' It's not fair. I deserve a perfect body. They owe it to me."

"It must have been hard," I commiserated. "What else was it like for you back on earth?"

"Boring. How could it have been otherwise? I was a secretary tucked away in a corner, endlessly typing. They didn't want me as a receptionist. Clients don't want to see a fat person. They don't want fat salespeople. Men didn't want to date me. Women were embarrassed to be seen with me."

"And now you're bored here too," I pointed out.

But she didn't really get the point. "Of course," was all she could say. "You'd think at least they would provide some entertainment. There's not even a television."

"I suppose you haven't tried going outside?" I asked. It was only a half-question, since I anticipated the answer.

"No. Why should I? People would just see me as fat . . . the way you do," she added accusingly.

I stated the obvious. "So you're sort of stuck."

"That's what Rebecca and Jonathan keep saying. And you'll say it too, won't you? That my body's just a projection now. That I can change it. That if I work to change the way I think, I can change my projection. That I think of myself as twenty-five, so I project myself that way. So if I think of myself as thin, then I will look thin. Or I don't have to project myself at all. Will you make love to me?"

I experienced an extraordinary set of reactions. The first was surprise at what seemed a total non sequitur—suddenly asking me out of nowhere whether I'd make love with her. The next was its opposite. It struck me that the question, bizarre though it seemed, might be striking to the heart of the matter. Then I began to feel awkward about not answering her with a quick affirmative, as if my gallantry were somehow at stake. This was followed by a wave of anger for putting me in such a predicament.

"See," Tish almost screeched. "I disgust you, don't I? I disgust you."

My anger stood me in good stead. "Please be decent enough to give me time," I commanded.

She obeyed while I continued to think. It was correct that she disgusted me physically. Only now, at a deeper level than I ever had before, I began to question what physicality was all about. Was it not all about projection in a sense? Several occasions back on earth I'd had intense erections with women who had not been at all beautiful in the world's terms and had been impotent with several others who'd been overtly gorgeous. Sex was, at least in part, like sleep, a matter of the soul.

I'd entered this room because I'd sensed through its walls an intense loneliness. That loneliness was real, whether Tish wanted to acknowledge it or not. The healer in me desired to heal it. If that meant making love to her, maybe I could, not with my projected body; it couldn't even feel, but with my soul. Was it possible for souls to intermingle, to copulate in some fashion? I suspected it might be if I tried.

There were two problems, however. One was simply that I was not attracted to her soul. It did not disgust me as did her body, but there was no desire for it. Tish had said she was bored—bored here and bored back on earth. And that was what I felt about her soul; it was unrelievedly bored and, because it was, it was also boring. Tish wished for TV in her room. That was one of the features of earth I definitely did not miss. During my later years almost all of its programming had bored me to tears. I had a profound sense that attempting to copulate with Tish's soul would be like forcing myself to watch a game show.

Still, I could do it if it might help. But would it? What would be the effect of my fondling her soul? It might terrify her. Or she might enjoy it. And if she enjoyed it—if being made love to made her feel pretty or gave her a surcease of loneliness—she would cling onto it. And me. She would want it over and again like an addict with his heroin. I would become her fix, and she would try to chain me to herself.

"No," I said finally. "I will not make love to you. Yes, your projected body is a turn-off to me because it's fat. But it's only a projection, and projections can't make real love. The reason it's taken me so long to answer is I've been wondering if it would be possible for us to make *real* love, for our souls to actually couple. I don't know if it is possible. I wouldn't know unless I tried. But I've decided not to try. And the reason I don't want to try has nothing directly to do with your weight. You said that your Greeters, Rebecca and Jonathan, keep telling you that you're stuck, and I agree with them. I think that making love with you would be like being stuck along with you, and frankly, I don't want to be stuck."

"Oh, go away," Tish said.

"Soon," I responded, "but would you mind if I ask you a few questions first?"

Tish assented.

"It sounds as if Rebecca and Jonathan have visited you more than once," I commented. "How many times have they been to see you here?"

"Three. They come whenever I ask them to."

"And you haven't left here yet yourself?"

"No. I told you that already." Tish sounded annoyed.

"Am I the only other person besides your Greeters who's visited you?"

"Yes."

"My Greeters told me they'd been assigned to me," I noted. "Is that what they told you too?"

"Yes."

"Did they suggest one of the reasons they were specifically assigned to you was because they have such perfect body projections?"

"Something of the sort."

"What did they do when they were back on earth?"

"I don't know," Tish said. "I didn't ask them. I'm not a nosy person like you are. They keep asking me questions. And talking about changing. All the time. Changing and projections. Changing, changing, changing. They're boring."

I—my projected body—stood up to go. "My Greeters told me they'd been to a school for Greeters. I think maybe it was a very good school, Tish, because they struck me as quite skilled. Certainly I did not find them boring. Yes, people are very different, but I'd like to suggest you listen to them the next time Rebecca and Jonathan visit you. I make that suggestion because I get a feeling that listening doesn't come easily to you."

"It doesn't come easily to *you*, you mean." Tish almost spat. "I thought I'd told you to leave."

I wished myself straight back to my room. The green was a relief. I wasn't sure I cared if I ever saw pink again.

The Pink Purgatory. When I'd asked Norma and Sam whether this was heaven, hell, or purgatory, they'd replied, "Take your pick." I still didn't know whether it was heaven for me. The Adjustment sounded closer to the mark. But I felt as if I'd just had a clear vision of purgatory. Tish did not seem to be in hell, at least not as one might think of hell. There were no flames or pitchforks, no torture, not even tribulation in the ordinary sense of the word. Indeed, she had a room of her favorite color and apparently free psychotherapy whenever she wanted it. Still she was miserable in her own way. And it most definitely was her pick. She was doing her very best to fight the Adjustment, and the bars of her boring cell were of her own making.

On the other hand, if Tish had made this place a purgatory for herself, how could anyone make a hell out of it? That had me curious . . . and uneasy. I wasn't sure I wanted a vision of hell.

I felt tired. This surprised me. It didn't seem that long since I'd awoken. But then it occurred to me I'd done quite a bit of exploring in a short time and had more adventures and experiences and learning than most people had in a full day. It also occurred to me that Tish was tiring. I recalled how we psychotherapists had invented the term "burnout"—for ourselves. And how what had caused my own burnout after less than twenty years was not the tragedy in my .patients' lives but their attachment to it, the same sort of "stuckness" Tish demonstrated. They all entered therapy claiming they wanted to change, but no sooner was it under way than they started behaving as if the last thing on God's earth they wanted to do was change. Resistance, we called it. Often it felt like too mild a word for trying to push boulders uphill. In that respect, Tish was no surprise. What was so tiring about her rationalizations, her inflexible attachments, her denial, her stubborn disinterest, was that I'd seen them all before. The only thing surprising was that she'd been transferred lock, stock, and barrel—all three-hundred-plus pounds of her—from my old office up here.

Maybe that's a definition for purgatory, I thought: when one moves from life on earth to the afterlife and acts as if nothing had changed.

Sam and Norma had told me their role was to assist me in the Adjustment. I would call upon them again if for no other reason than to thank them for their skill and professionalism. Did they have clients like Tish, I wondered? If so, I felt sorry for them. Certainly I did not envy Rebecca and Jonathan. As far as any adjustment went, Tish seemed determined to fight it tooth and nail every step of the way. I'd guessed correctly that Rebecca and Jonathan and their young and perfect bodies had been assigned to her so as to demonstrate that someday she too could have a beautiful projection. Now an additional reason occurred to me. Undoubtedly their projections were youthful because they were young in spirit. Perhaps their youthfulness made them immune to burnout.

It was along about then I fell asleep praying for Tish, and praying for Jonathan and Rebecca, that they, this pair I'd never met, would somehow succeed in wearing her down before she wore them out.

CHAPTER

6

On this morning—if it was morning—I awoke with eagerness for the first time since my forties. I was facing only adventure. Nothing to do except explore. Without having to floss my teeth or exercise my back, without even having to reach for my cigarettes, I was amazed how quickly I was ready. In no time I wished myself out of my little green room into the gray corridor.

Yesterday—if it was yesterday—I'd gone to the right. So today let's go left! I leaped a hundred feet. Then another. And that was when I stopped in surprise. About thirty feet farther ahead next to the corridor wall there was a trash can.

My surprise was threefold. Yesterday I'd wished for some kind of detritus—anything—to relieve the drabness of the corridor. Today I'd expected only that same drabness. The perversity of the human mind is striking. Give me a single experience of a particular situation and I somehow automatically assume it will be that way forever.

But why should there be any detritus anyway? Was this

not a place of pure spirit where all that looked material, like bodies and walls, were but projections? We souls here did not eat; we did not defecate; we produced no garbage. So why now suddenly should there be a garbage can? It made no sense. Perhaps the can itself was a projection of mine, but I could discern no reason I should project something I'd not been expecting, something that was the furthest from my mind.

What was most surprising of all was its ordinariness. It didn't belong here but it very much belonged back on earth. Maybe it was my projection; it looked exactly like ones we'd had that Mary Martha and I had purchased at Sears. Three feet high, its apparently plastic walls were that typical olive green and the lid a typical black cover secured by typically movable metal handles.

I giggled. I was not accustomed to opening strange garbage cans to view their contents, but I was not about to leave this one alone. I moved over to it, imagining its handles flipping down and the lid flipping off. That's precisely what happened. The lid fell to the floor and I looked in. To my amazement all I could see were small brown rocks, rough but round, each about three inches in diameter. Yet even more amazing was what I felt. I felt miserable. Wave upon wave of misery swept through me.

Here my training as a psychiatrist served me well. I'd learned that not all of my feelings originated within myself. If I suddenly felt uneasy walking down a dark street maybe it was because something was lurking down an alley to *make* me feel uneasy. When I felt particularly worried with a particular patient there was usually something about him to cause me to worry even though I might not yet be able to put my finger on it. In this case I had a strong sense that there was something inside the trash can underneath the rocks that was giving me this miserable feeling. Specifically, I sensed that the misery resided not so much in my mind as inside the waste receptacle itself.

I wanted to uncover it. Driven both by my curiosity and my almost compulsive desire to "cure" misery of any sort, I wished one of the rocks out of the can. I watched it rise up, noiselessly fall to the floor of the corridor, and immediately evaporate. Instantly another rock materialized to take its place in the container. Simultaneously I heard a voice. "Excuse me, sir," it pronounced, "but these rocks are not to be removed. Doing so is a violation of the Principle of Freedom, Section 43, Paragraph b."

"I'm sorry," I quickly responded. "No harm intended. I was just curious." I recalled Norma and Sam telling me that the Principle of Freedom governed this level of existence. "I'm a newcomer here," I went on to explain. "I don't want to violate anyone's freedom. It's just that I don't know all the rules yet."

"Certainly, sir." The voice—or soul—communicating was polite like that of a butler willing to overlook a minor faux pas. Like a butler it also invited no intimacy.

Nevertheless my curiosity was much too intense for me not to inquire further. "My name's Daniel Turpin. Would you mind telling me yours?"

"Robert Brown."

A prosaic name, I thought. "Could you tell me something more about yourself?" I asked.

"There's nothing much to tell, sir."

"But what are you doing in there underneath the rocks?"

"Doing? I'm one of the security guards, of course."

"What is it that you're guarding?"

"The Company."

"The Company?"

"Yes, sir. Amalgamated Systems."

"And what does Amalgamated Systems do?"

"It's a business, of course."

"Yes, but what kind of business?"

"I don't think I'm equipped to answer that, sir. I'm just a security guard. I believe it best you speak with the Director of Public Relations. Let me see if he's available."

It is possible to be aware of only so many feelings at one time. I suppose that the intense feeling of misery I had had from what was emanating from beneath the rocks was still with me, but my consciousness of it was eclipsed by a mixture of confusion and disorientation. As I began to analyze this, what initially struck me was the bizarre quality of the situation. Unless I had become totally insane, it seemed that I was communicating through a bunch of rocks with representatives of some sort of commercial enterprise existing at the bottom of a trash container in an otherwise empty corridor. I was hardly beginning to come to terms with the craziness of it all when my musing was interrupted by a new and different voice. "Hi, there," it said. It sounded jovial, friendly, outgoing. "I'm Henry Smith, Director of Public Relations. What can I do for you?"

Tucking away in my mind the fact that this man's name was as common as that of the first, I explained that I was a newcomer to this level of existence and that in the process of starting to explore my new world I'd inadvertently stumbled upon some sort of business operation the security guard told me was called Amalgamated Systems. "Naturally, I'm curious. Would you mind if I asked you some questions?"

"Of course not. Why should I? That's my job. Everything about the operations of Amalgamated Systems is a matter of public record."

"What is Amalgamated Systems exactly?" I asked.

"You are a newcomer, aren't you?" Mr. Smith exclaimed. There was no hint of disparagement in the rhetorical question; if anything only a hint of apology. "We tend to assume that everyone knows about Amalgamated Systems, but of course that's not the case, is it? We're not necessarily the center of the universe, are we? But then we tend to forget that from time to time, don't we? What are we? Well, we're a holding company, so to speak."

"Meaning a company that owns other companies?"

"That's it!" Mr. Smith said approvingly. "You hit the nail right on the head."

"And how many companies does Amalgamated Systems own?" I inquired.

"Twenty-four. An even two dozen! Unfortunately, that's the extent we're limited to by antitrust legislation."

I wondered how far the law could be stretched. "It is possible for a holding company to own other holding companies?"

"You're a smart one, aren't you? Yes, three of our companies are themselves holding companies. Again, that's the extent the law allows."

I felt I'd wandered off into a miasma of the conglomerate world that hadn't even intrigued me back on earth the way it had seemed to intrigue many. I needed to be grounded by the basics. "What kinds of things do some of your companies make?" I asked.

Mr. Smith gave a chuckle. "They all make money," he answered.

I appreciated the humor. I assumed he was assuring me with some pride that all the divisions of Amalgamated Systems were operating at a profit. "Good for you," I responded, "but what are some of their products?"

"Products? Products?" For a second I thought Mr. Smith might be confused. He was quick to point out, however, that I was the one who was confused. "You can't be *that* much of a newcomer. You wouldn't be wandering around asking questions if you didn't already realize there's nothing material here. There's nothing to make products out of, and even if there were there wouldn't be much demand for them. Without bodies people don't need toilets and faucets, soaps or cosmetics, clothes or foodstuffs."

"But what do your companies make?"

"I told you. They make money. They're all finance companies of one sort or another. Each has its own flavor, of course. Some specialize in the buying and selling of stocks, others in bonds. Some in low-risk and others in high-risk investments. One specifically in options. Naturally, our holding companies specialize in mergers and acquisitions. A lot of legal work is required there. In fact, it so happens that one of our companies is a corporate law firm."

I felt dazed. I recollected back on earth how some people criticized the financial industry for the fact it didn't produce anything; it only made money. But Mr. Smith was right. What other kind of industry could there be here? Still, it was not an industry I was very familiar with. I too once had made money as a psychiatrist and then as an author or lecturer in what I suppose would be called the service industry. Maybe "the entertainment industry." Nevertheless I'd had a product of sorts. Yet wasn't the financial industry also a service industry? Certainly I'd used it to serve me: to structure my professional corporation, to prepare my income taxes, to advise me on investments, to manage my pension plan, and to send me all those statements each month. The fact of the matter, however, was that I'd never made enough money to become all that deeply involved, and the financial industry remained a shadowy world for me. Nevertheless as I thought about it now, questions began to bubble up in my mind—formed, half-formed, and some still inchoate.

I asked the most obvious one first. "Money is in some ways abstract. But we have symbols for it. Dollar bills. Bankbooks. Stock certificates. We even joke that it's all paper. Yet you correctly pointed out there's nothing material here. That means there's no paper. And no ink. And no adding machines. No computers. How do you keep track of all the money?"

Mr. Smith practically congratulated me upon my acumen. "A very good question, and it is a problem indeed. The only way to surmount it is to use people. A large percentage of our employees spend their full time devoting themselves to keeping the ever changing numbers in their heads. Even though we always round off to the nearest dollar, it's an extremely inefficient use of manpower."

My initial sense of the misery from beneath the rocks returned. "God, that must be awful," I commiserated, "to have to spend all one's time calculating and remembering numbers!"

"Oh, to the contrary," Mr. Smith reassured me. "Most of us love it. Certainly everyone here. People like counting. We have an extremely high level of job satisfaction at Amalgamated Systems."

The world as I had known it seemed very far away. Ever since I had been here, however long it was, I'd not even thought of money. Nevertheless I could clearly remember the almost perverse delight I'd taken back on earth counting my gains. At moments of anxiety or depression I would compulsively review our portfolio in my mind, usually finding solace that the numbers were by and large increasing. Yes, I could understand how people might take pleasure in counting money. But it was not a trait in myself that I'd particularly admired. Even then it was only an occasional activity for me. I still felt sorry for people who had to do it all day long.

Another question was obvious. "Since there are no real products here," I asked, "why bother? Why bother to make money since there's nothing to spend it on?"

"Oh, there are things to buy," Mr. Smith assured me. "Other companies, for instance. Amalgamated Systems might sell off one of its divisions to a smaller company. That would then leave room for us to use our profits to buy an even larger company than the one we'd sold. I'm not saying we're doing that at the moment. The distribution of insider information is prohibited. It's just an example. But there are always deals to be made."

"Why?" I persisted. "You imply you might want to grow larger; I suppose Amalgamated Systems can make still more money. Is that what it's all about? Growth for the pure sake of growth?"

"Of course."

"I may be naive," I said, "but I'm still not sure I understand to what end you want to grow in wealth when there's nothing to spend it on except to keep growing."

"Oh, I doubt you're naive, Mr. Turpin," the response came back through the rocks. "You're just playing the devil's advocate, so to speak. Ha, ha. We grow at the expense of other companies. Competition. That's what it's all about. That's what makes people tick."

Mr. Smith had said this with such certainty, I suspected it was what made him tick. And possibly everyone at Amalgamated Systems. Still, I was less than satisfied. "How is it that competition motivates so many?" I inquired. "On earth it seemed that people were competing for money because they were really competing for possessions and physical security. But here, as far as I can ascertain, there don't seem to be any possessions in the ordinary sense, and since we don't have any bodies none of us have to worry about starving. So why compete?"

Mr. Smith laughed. "You really are a philosopher, aren't you? Like Socrates going around asking questions all the time, even when you already know the answers. You know why we compete. It's for status and power."

It had hardly been that self-evident to me. "Who's the president of Amalgamated Systems?" I queried.

"Mr. Frank Jones."

First a Brown; then a Smith; and now a Jones. It was too much of a coincidence. They were pseudonyms, I supposed—fake names. Why? But I chose not to press the point.

I wanted to continue with my line of thought. "So Mr. Jones must have a great deal of status and power," I commented.

"Oh, yes, indeed."

"How did he get to be president?"

"Oh, I'm afraid that's protected information, sir. Principle of Freedom, Section 137, Article 4."

Why did I have the feeling the numbers had just been made up? Yet what would be the point of a challenge? "Okay," I said, "but what sort of things does Mr. Jones do with all his power?"

"Well, he never operates alone of course. He's always consulting with the board of directors and his vice-presidents. He's known to be a very modern manager. An enlightened leader, as we refer to him. But he does have the biggest say in which companies are bought and which are sold. And of course in the promotion or demotion of top employees."

"Since status is such a motivator," I remarked, "I'd gather a lot of your employees must be scrambling pretty hard for promotions and running pretty scared about being demoted."

"No more than in any other business," Mr. Smith was quick to point out. "Less so, in fact. Indeed, we have a saying here that 'At Amalgamated Systems we're one big happy family!' "

I straightened up to take stock. Emptying my mind of questions for the moment, I concentrated on feeling. I had the same feeling of misery. It was just as strong. As was my sense that the misery was emanating from underneath the rocks. Only this time, as I analyzed it, I could discern that a major component of the misery was terror—sheer, human terror.

Having straightened, I looked as far as I could down the corridor. There was nothing to be seen. No additional trash cans. "Where are your companies located?" I asked.

"Located?" For the first time Smith sounded confused.

"Yes. Where do all your employees work?"

"In here, of course. All the companies are right in here."

"Inside this single can?" My voice expressed astonishment, but at least I had the gentility to not specify it as "trash can."

"Oh, yes. Souls don't take up much space, you know. It's one of the real pluses of business operations here. We don't have to worry about plant or plant design or architecture and all that. A considerable relief."

"How many employees do you have in there?" I asked.

The answer was instantaneous. "One hundred and forty-three thousand, eight hundred and twelve as of this morning. We're a Fortune One Thousand company," Mr. Smith added with obvious pride.

Had I believed him for certain, I would have been simply aghast. As it was, an entire range of feelings tumbled through me, one upon another: astonishment, anger, pity, skepticism, and confusion. Above all, confusion, although I should have become accustomed to being confused by now in this strange new world. Granting souls might not take up space in the ordinary sense of the word, how could over a hundred thousand of them possibly exist underneath some rocks in the bottom of a single garbage can? I doubted even maggots could do that, eating each other up in the process. "They all work together in there?" I repeated, not even hiding my horror.

"Oh, yes."

"But where do they live?"

"Live? They live in here, of course."

"Where are their homes? Where do they go home to at night?"

"This is their home," Mr. Smith insisted.

"But my god, man, where do they sleep?"

"Sleep?" Mr. Smith echoed. "Excuse me. I forgot how new you are. We don't sleep here."

Now it was my turn to echo. "You don't sleep?"

"No. At least not those of us in business. We can't afford to."

"What do you mean, 'You can't afford to'?"

"Just that. We're all too busy, for one thing. It's not just the volume, the sheer volume of calculations, and the pace of operations. It's a matter of attention. If we didn't pay attention we might let something slip. A deal, for instance. We might let a deal slip through our fingers. Particularly since someone is always trying to sneak one over us."

"Someone in another company?"

"That too. But as likely a coworker. As I said, we're one big happy family here at Amalgamated Systems, but that doesn't mean we're not competitive. This is business. Either you keep up or you go under. As an individual and as an organization. It's a dog eat dog world, you know."

What disturbed me the most, of course, was this matter of not sleeping. How could people not sleep? And had not Sam and Norma reassured me that souls need to sleep too? I would have totally discredited Mr. Smith save for a small turn of phrase he'd used. When I'd echoed, "You don't sleep?" with such amazement, he'd replied, "No. At least not those of us in business." I suddenly recalled a sight I'd witnessed many times. As a lecturer I'd crisscrossed the country over and over for twenty years and spent a sizable portion of my life in airports. I usually wrote while waiting for my flights, but it was never frantic and I could not fail to note the occasional man—they somehow all looked the same—who stood at the phone until the very last moment before his flight, dialing and redialing. He always spoke rapidly and loudly enough for me to be certain he was making deals. And it had always struck me that he was in the grip of an addiction—perhaps a demon—the demon of deal making. He had never looked either happy or unhappy, but he had always looked as if he was sweating slightly despite the air conditioning. Yes, I could conceivably understand how someone in the grip of such an addiction might not want to sleep, might not even be able to sleep, just as a rat will starve itself to death if you allow it to press a lever that will stimulate the pleasure center in its brain.

Something else about his phrasing allowed me to believe that Mr. Smith was possibly speaking the truth—in this regard if no other. It was his sense of normalcy. He was clearly aware that I was both a newcomer and an outsider. And that not everyone here was in business, as he construed business. Yet just as clearly he evidenced his certainty that he and his coworkers were utterly normal, and that their lifestyle in the barrel was the norm. Without even trying, he'd expressed an attitude that I didn't quite "get it" yet. And that if I came to my senses I'd obviously choose to be one of them. It didn't feel like a trick. It felt more like we were conversing out of totally different frames of reference. I changed my tack somewhat. "Why are you hidden behind rocks?" I asked.

"Why?" he answered. "We wish to remain unseen, of course."

"So I gather. But why?"

"You really are a strange one, aren't you?" Mr. Smith commented. "Think about business back on earth. Occasionally you'd see some businessman who was flamboyantly public. A Lee Iacocca or a Donald Trump. But they were the exceptions, and rather stupid if you don't mind me saying so. A good businessman will play his cards close to his chest. He won't advertise his salary. Outside the company he'll be as anonymous as possible. People are out to get you, but they can't get you if they don't know who you are."

"I guess I understand."

Mr. Smith picked up on the dubious note in my voice. "That's not the only reason for anonymity. We have industrial secrets, you know. How the others would like to get ahold of them! As it is, we have to be constantly on our guard against industrial espionage."

I had little doubt that Amalgamated Systems had its own staff of spies. "How do you know that I'm not a spy?" I inquired. "For that matter, why do you talk to me at all?"

"The Principle of Freedom requires it. Although the Principle allows us the freedom to generally preserve our anonymity, it also allows people such as yourself the freedom to know of our existence and make reasonable inquiries. As you've undoubtedly gathered, one of my jobs is to know the regulations so well as to determine which inquires are reasonable and which are not. Of course we want to give the public the maximum amount of latitude. As our president always says, there's nothing more important than good public relations."

I chose not to ask Mr. Smith why Mr. Jones thought public relations so important. As far as I was concerned, their PR had done nothing to make Amalgamated Systems appealing. To the contrary, it sounded like my idea of a nightmare. Consequently, I questioned how people joined it.

"Unless they come from another company," Smith told me, "they're referred here for employment by their Greeters."

I was thunderstruck. I couldn't imagine people like Norma and Sam referring anyone to the bottom of a trash can. "Why do the Greeters refer them?"

"I'm afraid that is protected information, Mr. Turpin. Section 119, Paragraph c."

"But my Greeters didn't refer me," I protested. "I've got a room hundreds of times larger than your can, a room all to myself. They never even mentioned any business to me. Not Amalgamated Systems, not any business. Why would they refer someone here?"

"All I can tell you, Mr. Turpin, is that everyone who comes here is a volunteer. They *want* to work here. We are not a slave camp, Mr. Turpin."

"But why?" I persisted. "Why would anyone volunteer to be squeezed under rocks in the bottom of a can?"

"I'm terribly sorry I can't answer you, sir." I'd expected Mr. Smith might likely be irritated by my persistence, particularly with its implied criticism. He was quite unruffled, however, and even ingratiating in an oily fashion. "You could, of course, ask your Greeters themselves, but other than that suggestion I'm afraid I can't be any more helpful. Principle of Freedom, you know; same section, same paragraph."

So I switched gears. "How many of your employees are women?"

"Well over a third. Amalgamated Systems is an Equal Opportunity Employer. Of course the percentage differs from subsidiary to subsidiary. Women tend not to be as attracted to accounting operations as the men. On the other hand, almost two-thirds of our legal division is female. Actually, another conglomerate has a subsidiary, Reputation Consultants, that's mostly made up by women."

I was curious. "Reputation Consultants? What does it do?"

"It's a consulting firm, of course. One of our executives might employ their services if he wanted to enhance his own reputation. Or more likely if he wanted to damage another executive's reputation. Women seem to have a particular sensitivity for reputation issues."

I wasn't sure this was true. For that matter, I wasn't sure that much of anything Mr. Smith told me was true. "I thought Amalgamated Systems was just one big happy family," I commented. "What's this about hiring a consultant to help you damage a coworker's reputation?"

"No reason not to if you can afford it. Competition, remember? We're all after status and power. But that doesn't mean we don't all pull together. Of course we do. It's like the good old U.S. of A. The politicians have their reputation-damage consultants, don't they? And the system works just fine."

"It wasn't clear to me when I left how well it was still working," I interjected. Not wanting to be sidetracked by the vagaries of political opinion, however, I kept my focus on the business. "What happens when an executive's reputation gets seriously damaged?"

"He gets demoted, naturally."

"Does he ever get fired?"

"Heavens, no. We don't fire here. There's always a place for someone with Amalgamated Systems."

"Can he leave?"

"You mean go to another company? Of course. Everyone's free to work where they want. The executive search firms are very active here."

"Executive search firms?"

"Yes. Headhunters, they were nicknamed back on earth. We conglomerates routinely steal—hire away—executives from each other."

Suddenly I became aware of feeling a strange exhaustion. Mr. Smith and I hadn't been talking for more than thirty minutes, yet it seemed to me like thirty hours. If I didn't get away soon I felt I would die. Still, Smith's answer to my last question had only been partial, and I needed the other part. "You've been most kind and patient with me," I said, "and I don't want to take up much more of your time. But when I asked whether someone could leave Amalgamated Systems, you answered in terms of leaving to work for another company. Could he just leave business completely? Quit your world altogether?"

"You mean drop out?" For the first time I detected a note of anxiety in Smith's voice.

"Yes, I suppose you could call it that, but to me it would be more like dropping in since he or she would be coming from your world into mine. Are your employees free to do that?"

"I told you they're volunteers. That means they're free."

I could definitely tell Smith was being evasive now. I bored in. "How many drop out? How many a year?"

"Oh, it's very rare, practically unheard of."

"How many a year, Mr. Smith? On the average?"

"Two and seven tenths a year. That's an attrition rate of less than 0.0002 percent. There's no company on earth that can come anywhere near our retention rate. I keep telling you, Mr. Turpin, that Amalgamated Systems is a happy family. We have extraordinary job satisfaction here."

"That is remarkable," I agreed. "It sounds like you're to be congratulated. I know it's a very small point, but why is it that those mere two to three a year do drop out?"

"Why? How should I know? They don't make any sense."

"You may not understand it, Mr. Smith. I don't expect you to agree with them. But what is it that those very few say as to why they're dropping out?"

"I'm sorry but that information is protected. Principle of Freedom, Section 7, Article 13."

"I'm going now, Mr. Smith. Do you want me to put the lid back on?" My question was not simply metaphorical.

"No, I'll do it. Goodbye, Mr. Turpin. And come back to visit us again anytime you like."

At that the black lid, which all this time had been lying on the floor of the gray corridor, lifted itself through the air and landed on top of the can. The metal handles rose up and secured it into place. I fervently wished myself back into my little green room and instantly was there.

Several times during my life back on earth I'd been too exhausted to sleep. I first had to read, have a drink, or do something to relax enough for my fatigue to take its natural course. This was a similar occasion. I needed time to contemplate, to get some semblance of understanding of all that had just happened to me.

I began by contemplating my own exhaustion. Why was it so dramatic? The answer that came to me was unreality.

I'd not merely been having a dialogue with an invisible representative of an invisible organization; I'd been wrestling with unreality.

The most unreal part—that 140,000-odd souls were living and working in the bottom of a trash can—for all I knew was the most real. I sensed that Mr. Smith was a profound liar, and if there were all those souls in there they probably were too. There was nothing he said I could declare with certainty was a lie. Yet everyone's name seemed fake. He seemed to number regulations out of thin air. All was kept unseen. Answers to crucial questions were classified "protected." Several times he was grossly evasive. I frankly had no idea what was true and what wasn't or how to tell which portion was real and which unreal.

The unreality of it all was squared by the likelihood Mr. Smith didn't even know that he was lying. I had consulted with a few large corporations while on earth where some of the top executives truly believed that their company was "one big happy family" when the reality was that most of the employees were angry, frightened, bitter, and deeply dissatisfied. Still, while they were hardly happy campers, I did not sense during my visits to those corporations anything like the sense of collective misery I'd felt emanating through the rocks from the souls at the bottom of the trash can.

Indeed, the sense was so powerful that the misery of the employees of Amalgamated Systems was the only thing seeming to me to be real for sure. How could they possibly be volunteers? How could less than one in ten thousand of them leave each year? I recalled thinking that Mr. Smith seemed to have normal and abnormal all mixed up, that vicious competition for meaningless status and power was the norm, that he and his coworkers were the normal ones and that I was the outsider, the deviant. And that was when I remembered Stephanie.

Stephanie had come to see me in my early days as a psychiatrist back on earth. She sought my services because she was miserable, extremely depressed, although she had no idea why. Her depression was so severe she could hardly talk, and getting her to verbalize her thoughts and feelings was like pulling teeth. One afternoon when she was typically almost mute I thought I might use the fact that it was the Christmas season to help her open up. "Tell me about Christmas when you were a child," I instructed.

"There's nothing to tell."

I knew she was an only child, and as yet I had no handle on her parents. I thought it best to be more specific. "Remember back to when you were ten," I told her. "I want you to tell me what Christmas was like in your family when you were ten years old."

"But there's nothing to tell," she insisted. "It was an ordinary, average, normal Christmas."

It was my turn to be insistent. "Let me be more precise. What exactly did you do on Christmas eve?"

"It was just a normal, family Christmas eve," she protested.

"Damn it," I practically exploded. "What did you, Stephanie, *do* on Christmas eve between the hours of six and nine?"

"I wrapped the presents, of course."

"The presents you gave your parents?"

"Those too."

The first alarm bells rang in my head. "Those too?" I repeated. "What did you mean, 'those *too*'?"

"I wrapped all the presents."

"All the presents?"

"Yes, the presents I gave them, the presents they gave me, and the presents they gave each other."

"You wrapped all the presents?" I repeated dumbly.

"Oh, yes, I bought them too," she added matter-of-factly.

Again I could only repeat in dawning horror, "You bought them too?"

"Sure. Right after Thanksgiving each year my father would give me twenty-five dollars and say, 'Here, take ten and get me a present for your mother, and ten to buy her one for me, and five for a present from us to you.' "

Slowly and silently tears began to trickle down my face. Stephanie noticed. "Why are you crying?" she asked in surprise.

"I guess I'm crying for you," I answered. "Literally for you because you're not able to cry for yourself yet."

That was when I first understood the origin of most neuroses. I suppose there are a few neuroses that result from a single trauma someone experienced in his or her life. Generally, however, the problem is a trauma that is repeated day in and day out or year after year with such frequency and regularity that the victim comes to perceive the trauma as no longer traumatic but normal. That is what had happened with Stephanie. She truly believed she'd had normal, average Christmases as a child. Only when that sort of trauma occurs routinely everything becomes mixed up: what's healthy comes to be defined as sick and the deranged can seem perfectly sane.

So, yes, I understood how Mr. Smith might have thought

that life in the bottom of the trash can was a thoroughly normal existence and how he probably regarded people like me with a mixture of scorn and pity. Not that I would diagnose him or his coworkers as simply neurotic. I suspected the sickness went even deeper than what we ordinarily mean by neurosis. Nevertheless the dynamic was the same. The intense misery of Amalgamated Systems was very real, but that didn't mean the poor employees considered themselves wretched and, yes, maybe, just maybe, there might be reasons they'd volunteer for it.

Yesterday—if it was yesterday—I'd wondered if my visit to Tish's pink room hadn't been a visit to Purgatory. Now, as I was finally drifting off it occurred to me that perhaps today I'd been standing at the gates of Hell . . . or at least one of its subdivisions.

CHAPTER

7

On this day I awoke with profound indecision. It was not unpleasant. Back on earth I would begin each day with a forty-five-minute period I called my prayer time. Enjoying my first two cigarettes with a great mug of coffee, I'd sit in bed relishing the early morning light and plotting the hours ahead of me. Although to an observer it would appear that I wasn't really doing anything, it was this period of contemplation that made it possible for me to succeed in doing more rather than less. It was when I fine-tuned my schedule, prioritizing my priorities so that I wouldn't have to spin my wheels. It was also when I asked God what my priorities ought to be, lest I waste time on matters of only seeming consequence. Of all my acquaintances, God was the best efficiency expert.

Only today I had far more options than on earth. One was to call for my Greeters, Sam and Norma. When I'd asked them whether this was heaven, hell, or purgatory, they'd answered, "Take your pick." Well, since then I suspected I'd had visions of purgatory and hell in that order, but I wasn't sure. I needed their verification. And, if verified, I had a hundred questions more. What could be done to help Tish get unstuck in her Pink Purgatory? Why would Greeters ever "refer" anyone to Amalgamated Systems? How did those very, very few get out of the trash can? And on and on and on.

But it was not my style to bother people unnecessarily, and all these questions could wait a little while at least. Norma and Sam had made it clear I was free to do much more exploring. I could, of course, continue to explore what lay in and off the gray corridor outside my little green room. God only knew what more I might discover. Yet brief though my forays had been, my feeling today was one of wanting to expand my horizons beyond this hotel.

There had been a kind of myth back on earth that when we got to the afterlife we could meet and converse with the great souls of the past. Whose company would I like to seek? Jesus, of course, but that seemed presumptuous. Abraham Lincoln? Same thing. I imagined that he was very much with Jesus, and I felt disinclined to invade their privacy. Shakespeare? C.S. Lewis? Eventually, if possible, that might be nice, but I had had the opportunity to meet a good many famous people during my life on earth, and celebrity seeking in and of itself held zero appeal for me.

No, the one person I most wanted to see was Mary Martha, my own un-famous, extraordinary wife; only now, here, she would be my ex-wife—not by divorce but by the liberation of death. Ours had been a vivid marriage of close to fifty years. I often wondered how we had survived the first thirty of them together. I was unfaithful, demanding, and over-controlling. She was possessive, temperamental, and vindictive. There were times it seemed we had invented the Battle of the Sexes all by ourselves for our own personal suffering.

The battle escalated with the advent of the Women's Movement. The woman with the name of Martha whom I'd married in 1949 formally changed her name to Mary in 1971. She accused me of being a male chauvinist pig, and was damned if she was going to be identified in any fashion with a Gospel woman who customarily slaved over a hot stove. Although a bit paranoid at times, she was not crazy; I was, in fact, a male chauvinist in certain ways.

We worked well together with the children. But even though we were both devoted to them, it was more than the children that kept us going. We had mutual determination, pertinacity, considerateness . . . and humor. It was difficult. It was also doubtful either of us could have lived with anyone else. Certainly we never stumbled across such a person.

By the time the children had grown and left, beautiful things had begun to happen. She'd come to realize there was a part of her that deeply enjoyed homemaking, and in 1980 she changed her name yet once more—this time finally to Mary Martha. Although never enamored of homemaking myself, under her tutelage I did manage to exorcise myself of most of my chauvinism. We came to accept each other's foibles and limitations, and then, oddly enough, we partially evolved out of them. We mellowed. Perhaps it was the diminution of our glands that allowed us to become softer, but our later years were enormous fun. Celebrating each other's separateness, our union paradoxically became one of almost mystical closeness.

Mary Martha loved flower gardens and constructed them with care wherever we lived. "I like to be surrounded by bright colors," she proclaimed. When she suddenly died from a stroke three years before me, I was not utterly bereft in the sense that many in my position might be. Over the decade before, helped by our capacity for psychological separation, we had each prepared for the other's death. Indeed, I was glad she had had at least an easy death and, until my cancer sapped all I had, over the next two years, I did some of my very best work. Nevertheless by that final decade she herself had become a flower garden, and when she died all the color went out of my life.

So, yes, I very much wanted to see Mary Martha again. But would she want to see me? Sam and Norma had made it clear she had the freedom not to. Given the final beauty of our marriage, I imagined she would, but then I couldn't be sure of anything in relation to Mary Martha, particularly after three years. Her changeability had been a part of her colorfulness. Besides, separation had been the major theme of our decades together. We had become experts at constructively pulling away, giving each other plenty of space when necessary, but it never became totally painless. Why would she want me in her life again when it inevitably meant another pulling away? Why would I want it, for that matter? In my anxiety and indecision, I recognized my own hesitance; I definitely wanted to see her, but I was hardly in a rush about it. Indeed, some instinct told me today was not the day, that I should wait softly for a while.

I had the same instinct about the one other person I definitely wanted to see here: our son Timothy. Mary Martha and I had had three children: Timothy; two years later a daughter, Vicky; and two years after that a second son, Marshall. It had been Marshall and Vicky who had been at my deathbed. It had been Mary Martha and I who had been at Timmy's. Timmy started bruising easily when he was fifteen. The diagnosis was acute myelogenous leukemia. Of course, we did the usual chemotherapy, but he was dead within days of reaching seventeen.

I could go on and on about the agony, the terror, and the mystery of it all, but what would be the point? The fact is that we got over it, Mary Martha and I, and, more slowly, we did our best to help Vicky and Marshall get over it. I guess the most important thing I can say about Timmy's fatal illness is that it was not a total surprise. We'd had premonitions of it. In a sense, the boy was too good: prematurely wise and detached. He wasn't more than six years old when Martha and I first talked about the ethereal quality he had, as if he had come from another planet, and our foreboding that he was not intended to be on earth for long.

Not that that made it any easier. Indeed, one of our pains was a sense of guilt that we might somehow have caused his early demise by unconsciously communicating our premonitions of it to him—a self-fulfilling prophecy. It was ridiculous, but parents in such a situation can cook up virtually anything to cause themselves guilt, and all Mary Martha's and my psychological sophistication did in the end was probably make it harder on us—and perhaps on Timmy as well. In any case, one of my joys of finding myself alive after "death" was the certainty that Timmy and Mary Martha were still alive as well. So I wanted to see him too. But having once given him up, I also had the same sort of reluctance to contact him again, and on this morning of indecisiveness also felt that it too could—and should—wait a little bit at least.

Norma and Sam had indicated I could go back to earth if I wanted to as long as I didn't interfere with anything. But where? There were a thousand options, and my indecisiveness continued unabated. For some reason I started humming an old spiritual in my mind. Its first line came to me: "Go where I send thee." Of course! Why not let God do the deciding? Without even stopping to think of the risks involved, I spontaneously prayed, "Lord, send me wherever You wish."

The result was terrifying. Instantly I was enveloped in clouds of orange gas that were whipping past me at a speed beyond my comprehension. When I was in the army, stationed in the Pacific, I'd been on the edge of the eye of a major typhoon. It had been awesome. The short, ordinarily sturdy tree in the backyard had not merely bent or swayed in the wind; it had swirled round and round like a top gone crazy, and I'd known the meaning of a whirlwind. On that level, this was similar, but magnified a thousandfold. Metaphorically, the experience of the typhoon had been almost unearthly. Now there was no metaphor. This in the literal sense was unearthly.

So in that sense I knew where I was. I was not on Earth. I was more or less on the surface of some other planet, although God only knew which planet of which system in which galaxy. I had no idea what the swirling gases were composed of or even whether they were hot or cold. Having no body I could not feel the wind or its temperature, thankfully, for I realized with absolute certainty that no body could survive here. No human. No insect. No bacterium or virus. It was the first time in my life that my scientific curiosity was completely overwhelmed. It occurred to me that I could ask God to lift me sufficiently above the surface of the planet so I could see it in perspective and study it a bit, perhaps even ascertain whether it was in the solar system. Instead, I prayed with fervor, "Lord, get me out of here. Take me back to my little green room. Please!"

And back I was, both grateful and humbled. With the peace and security of my room, my curiosity returned. I'd asked God to take me wherever She or He wanted, and He'd sent me to an uninhabited planet in outer space. Why? I had no way of knowing, but I knew the effects the experience had had upon me. Perhaps He had wanted those effects. I recalled how God, trying to convey His power, had spoken to Job "out of the whirlwind." A picture is worth a thousand words, they say, and He had shown me the whirlwind. And had been there with me in it, for He had brought me right back when I begged Him, had He not?

What if He had not? What if He'd left me there? What if I'd gone there right straight from my deathbed? Instead, I had my little green room whenever I needed or wanted it. I suppose the two go together, but much as I was impressed by the power of it all, I was even more awed by the graciousness of God.

So I'd been to outer space! I'd never had the slightest yearning to be an astronaut, but as a physician and theologian I'd been almost as intrigued as anyone over the question of whether life existed on some other planet. I still had no answer to the question. But the experience of the utter uninhabitability of a single other planet gave me a far deeper appreciation than I'd ever had of the extraordinary hospitableness of the planet Earth. I recalled a drive Mary Martha and I had taken forty years before through the desert lands of eastern Washington state. It had been an atrociously hot summer day on our way with infant children to the west coast for assignment overseas. We had nicknamed the area Agony Gulch. But a few people lived in it here and there along with innumerable other assorted creatures—snakes, lizards, insects, an occasional cactus—and now that my eyes had just been opened, I saw Agony Gulch as a veritable oasis relative to the rest of the universe.

My indecisiveness of the morning had evaporated. I had no wish to further explore outer space, but I had a definite inclination to return to verdant earth if for no other reason than to try out my "wings." I giggled at the expression. Was I an angel, I wondered? Whether I was or wasn't, it was clear I wanted to prove I could return to earth and I chose the most verdant spot I could think of. I wished myself back to the rambling old New England colonial house Mary Martha and I had dwelled in for most of our marriage.

It was mid-June, I could tell. The foxgloves were in full bloom, as well as a plethora of other flowers—the time that Mary Martha's gardens were at their very best. This timing intrigued me. I'd died in early June, and it felt to me as if about a week had passed since. It seemed that perhaps there was at least some correspondence between God's time and earthly time.

We'd sold the house a decade before to move into a condo in a retirement village. It was a sensible decision. We no longer needed such a large home and the upkeep had become burdensome, as had the lengthy drives to and from the doctors and hospitals upon which we were increasingly dependent. But it was sad, not so much because the sale was such a distinct rite of passage into old age as the simple fact that we had loved the place. Floating around it now, I experienced a slight sense of disruption to see the new owners had built a swimming pool in the deep woods out back. But so what? Only the deer must have been inconvenienced, and I was happy to see that the flower gardens were being kept up.

I resisted the temptation to go inside the house. For one thing, I knew that would be where most of the changes would likely have occurred. For another, it felt to me it would be an invasion of privacy. Probably I need not have worried about the latter because I shortly had a disconcerting experience. I was "standing" on the side porch just off the kitchen, my back to the door, looking out over the flower gardens thinking of recounting to Mary Martha how well they were being maintained, when I sensed something happening behind me. I turned around just in time to see the wife of the couple we'd sold the place to—ten years older but quite recognizable—march out of the kitchen. It happened too quickly for me to even jump aside, and to my astonishment she walked right through me as she strode out into the garden. She walked through me! Until that moment I'd intellectually known I was now pure spirit, but this was the ultimate confirmation. I was invisible, empty of molecules, completely penetrable and utterly immaterial.

The experience helped me decide what to do next. As I'd emotionally separated from Mary Martha and Timmy—mostly—so had I from the other two children. But my old and often bad habit of caretaking still gripped me. It wouldn't hurt to visit Vicky and Marshall, would it? Just to check up on them? I knew it was foolish, that they were perfectly okay, and they would quite properly resent me for hovering over them . . . if they knew about it. With me bodiless and invisible, however, they wouldn't know.

I wished myself to Vicky first and quickly regretted it. She was with her husband, Tom, in the living room of their Des Moines home, and they were having a fight. Vicky was standing, her usual tall, blonde self, looking down at Tom, seated on the sofa. Tom was a large man, but seemed smaller as she berated him. "What do you mean, you don't know your schedule yet?" she snapped. "I told you last night we need to decide when we're going back east, and I reminded you about it this morning. 'Don't forget to be ready to give me a date when you get home,' I said. Didn't I?"

"I don't see what the hurry is," Tom protested.

"You know perfectly well that Marshall wants to set the memorial service as quickly as possible. And the sooner we go through the condo dividing up Dad's things, the sooner we can get it on the market."

"Well," Tom attempted to explain, "we don't have a partners' meeting until Friday. It can wait until then, can't it? I certainly didn't have the time today to go running around contacting each of them to find out the best time for me to take off."

Vicky pounced. "Then why didn't you tell me that last night or this morning?"

She was about to continue, but I was two thousand feet up in the air above her house looking down at the pretty little city and its river, having whisked myself well out of earshot. I had no desire to listen to them quarrel, and didn't know whether to laugh or cry. Yes, Vicky was okay, quite her old self. While I could have cried because it seemed a fight, I doubted that it seemed that way to either of them; they would have considered it normal discourse. They reminded me of my paternal grandparents whom I used to listen to squabbling over some hand of bridge they'd played thirty years before. "What were you doing bidding three no-trump?" my grandmother would demand. "What did you expect me to do when you opened with two hearts?" my grandfather would retort. Maybe it ran in the genes.

Yes, Vicky was okay. She was always nagging Tom, and Tom was always setting himself up for it, just as he had in this instance, as if he somehow liked to be berated. Which was surprising given the fact that he was a highly success-ful litigation lawyer, far more accustomed at work to be on the offense than the defense. Mary Martha had never been a nag, thank God, and we used to sorrowfully chuckle over the strange relationship between our daughter and son-in-law. And it wasn't just their relationship. Vicky had been a nag before she was twenty, and was always trying to nag us as well, although we never put up with it. But Tom took it placidly, and when she married him we suspected it was pre-cisely because he did take it—even seemed to invite it. So it goes. Our children are different from us. Since Vicky was a fine mother to our grandchildren, reserving her nagging for others, we'd had no reason to interfere.

And I had none now. Wordlessly saying goodbye to them for perhaps the final time, I wished myself to be with Mar-shall, imagining that he would be at his home in Los Ange-les where he was a film producer. Instead I found myself in a trailer at the end of a dusty road in New Mexico, amid the arroyos just north of Santa Fe. Tom was on location, playing his role in the filming of a western. He'd talked to me about it before I died. He'd been designing it to be untraditional. He was alone in the trailer, which was awash with scripts and film clips, and was writing away intensely on a yellow pad, deep in concentration. He was "into it," as they say. It was not just that he was working; he was having fun. He too was clearly okay, and again I wordlessly said my goodbye. Likely she already knew it, but if and when I saw Mary Martha I'd be able to report to her that, as far as the children were concerned, everything apparently was continuing to go along just fine.

Separation. Goodbye. Goodbye. Goodbye.

Still I was not quite ready to say goodbye to the earth and return to my little green room. I'd been flitting here and there. To where else could I flit? Anywhere, it appeared. If God could whisk me to another planet, surely I could skip continents. I wished myself to Tintagel on the southwestern coast of England.

It was no idle choice. Tintagel is the site of the ruins of an ancient castle built into the rugged Cornish bluffs that fall sharply into a tempestuous sea. The townspeople who reap profits from the visitors claim it to have been the castle of the legendary King Arthur, a claim for which there is no proof, but one not difficult to entertain given the romantic beauty of the spot. Mary Martha and I had visited it twice for its beauty, and I chose it now because it had been an old haunt of ours, a place in which we both had sensed an atmosphere of ancient holiness.

But that atmosphere was not present now. As I landed on the crumbling ramparts of the castle I found myself in the midst of a swarm of tourists. At first I dodged them but then, remembering my earlier experience at our old house, I just let them walk through me. It was disappointing. There is nothing like too many tourists to spoil the atmosphere of such a place, whether they are walking through you or not. An intriguing notion came to me, however. Maybe I could dispense with the tourists by altering my time. Not knowing it to be possible, I wished myself to the next morning, specifically to an hour after dawn, a time when there would be light to see by but before any visitors had arrived.

Immediately all was changed. The light was more dim with a hint of pink lingering in the clouds. I had what was left of the ramparts all to myself. As when we'd been there before, there was no sound except the wind rustling through the grasses inside the ruined walls, the ocean surging against the rocks far below, and the cry of an occasional solitary gull. I relished it, but not as I would had Mary Martha been sharing it once again with me. Still, I stayed a while, enjoying the magic of the place, amazed at its seeming timelessness.

Timelessness! Apparently I'd succeeded in moving myself forward a day in time. Could I move myself backward? How far? A day? A year? A century? A millennium? I couldn't imagine a more proper place for such an experiment. A millennium back would be the end of the tenth century. That was the time of the Viking raids, and it occurred to me that possibly the castle had been destroyed or deserted because of them. King Arthur was reputed to have reigned in the sixth century, but that was legend and quite possibly the castle hadn't yet been built. So I decided to compromise on the end of the eighth century.

It was a good choice. I found myself *inside* the castle. To my left was a rectangular room that was obviously the kitchen, lined by great fireplaces and huge iron cauldrons. To my right, perpendicular to the kitchen, was another large rectangular room which, with its long refectory table and banners on the wall, was just as obviously the banquet hall. In some ways it was primitive. The windows were small and, without candles, the banquet hall was almost dark. There was no door between it and the kitchen. Instead of chairs there were benches at the table. My greater impression, however, was how surprisingly civilized at least this part of the castle seemed. The ceiling of the hall was high, supported by well-hewn beams between which the ceiling had been painted bright orange. Unlike what I'd imagined, the room was spotlessly clean.

The place was bustling, given my presumption it was still only about an hour after dawn. Plainly dressed in skins, men and women of all ages scurried through the hall to and from the kitchen. Some were carrying cooked dishes. The king and queen—or prince and princess—were having breakfast in bed, I imagined. Their servants chattered with one another in a language which must have been a precursor of English but which was as incomprehensible to me as Czechoslovakian.

When I thought of further exploring the interior of the castle I had the same feeling as I'd experienced thinking about going inside Mary Martha's and my old house in New England; it felt like it would be an invasion of privacy. Besides, I bore in mind Sam and Norma's admonition to obey the Rule of Non-Interference when visiting earth, and in this case I would not only be intruding upon people's private domain but upon a whole different millennium. So I wished myself outside the castle to a spot two hundred feet above it.

The sight was all I'd hoped for. It was, as I'd previously only imagined from its tumbled ruins twelve hundred years later, much more than just a castle. There was a castle with a central courtyard on the isolated promontory. It rose close to a hundred feet high with its battlements on top. Surrounding it, however, were a dozen other substantial stone buildings, one a large chapel, and then a wide wall with its own battlements. On the other side of the isthmus to the promontory there was another great defensive battlement patrolled by two bowmen, relaxed yet clearly on the lookout over the moors. Were they looking for friend or foe, I wondered? Either, I supposed, and if for foe I imagined that Saxons would be the most likely candidates unless I had my centuries mixed up.

Suddenly I felt a wave of fatigue . . . and something akin to depression as well. I wished myself immediately back into my little green room. The transition was instant, but both feelings persisted.

The fatigue was easily explainable. Although the actual time had seemed short, it had been an extraordinarily full day when I thought about it. I'd been to another planet and then had to digest that little experience. I'd visited Mary Martha's and my old home and realized that people on earth could walk right through me. I'd checked up on both Vicky and Marshall. Then I'd not only bounced to another continent but learned I could move myself forward and backward in time. I could be a living time machine! Had I just not dropped in on the Dark Ages in Great Britain?

The freedom of it all should have been exhilarating. So why was I feeling depressed? The answer began to formulate itself as I contemplated my extraordinary lack of curiosity. Ordinarily I was an exploratory sort of person, eager to roam the frontiers of knowledge, hungry to discover new ideas and ferret out the underlying realities of history, physics, and all manner of other subjects. Yet I'd not even bothered to lift myself above the planet that God had placed me on to attempt to identify it. I'd not gone inside our old home. My checkups on Vicky and Marshall had been perfunctory. Had I further explored the castle I might have discovered whether King Arthur was a real historical figure or merely a mythical one. I could have whisked myself further back in time to study the prehistoric megalithic people of Great Britain who once had so intrigued me, and thereby solved the mystery of Stonehenge. For that matter, I could even have hopped over to Egypt and watched the pyramids being built. But I had done none of these things. Why not?

The reason, as I pondered the matter, was one of motive. My primary motive on this day had been to try out my wings: to see whether God could send me someplace; to see whether I could return to earth; to see whether at will I could go forward and backward in time. Beyond that the particulars were of little concern to me. The mysteries of King Arthur and Stonehenge were earthly concerns, and now I was a denizen of the afterlife they strangely held no fascination; I was quite content to let them be. Was I becoming incurious like Norma and Sam, I wondered?

So too it was with our old home. I'd gone there only as a place to start my visit back to earth. I no longer had any attachment to it, and hence little curiosity. Even Vicky and Marshall weren't major concerns to me. I grieved for the pains that each would have to suffer—would Vicky ever learn to not nag?—and I wished them well. But their lives were their own to lead, and I had finally and fully become what they had needed me to become: detached.

This was the cause of my mild depression, I realized. All my attachment to the earth was gone. This was right and proper, I knew, and ultimately cause for rejoicing. Here, wherever that might be, was, I suspected, where I belonged, my true Jerusalem. Still, there was this human sense of loss. I had lost my temporary roots on earth, and in this there was a certain poignancy if not sadness. It was quite possible I would never visit earth again or even care to. Still, I was free. If ever I did care to I could return to see all the things I'd missed out on.

Yes, I had tried my wings, and they'd worked amazingly well. Independent of space or time, I seemed more and more free to do as I wanted. But what was that? To what end was my freedom to be used? The question was so enormous I did the only thing I could have done; I fell asleep on it.

CHAPTER

8

Sleep is so gracious! Typical of my mild depressions, mine of yesterday had evaporated by the time I awoke. The huge question of what to do with my freedom lay unanswered, but I felt at peace with it. Meanwhile, lesser questions resurfaced with a vengeance. I may have become detached from my old world but my curiosity about this one had only intensified as a result of my brief experiences with it. How was it possible to move across space and time at will? How could I see without eyes, hear without ears, and think without a brain? Were heaven, hell, and purgatory merely states of mind?

My first inclination was to call for Norma and Sam, my Greeters. It was their role to help me with my Adjustment, and it seemed to me that these were proper questions of adjustment. I recalled, however, that I had already asked them, and the pair's answers had been vague and incomplete. Much as I appreciated their service, they themselves had made it clear they were unsophisticated souls who were comfortable acting with limited information. No, if it was possible, at this point I needed the most sophisticated mentor I could get. I prayed for such a person.

Within less than a minute there was a glow in the midst of my little green room. The glow had a center but its light extended outward so it was impossible to determine its boundaries. It also seemed to pulsate slightly. The light was predominantly white but within it there were ephemeral flickers of all the colors in the spectrum. I was reminded both of the flickering quality to Sam and Norma's projected bodies and the great light that had first met me upon my "death." This was something in between. It was, I instinctively knew, a being of great authority and wisdom. "Thank you for coming," was all I could say.

"You're welcome," it responded. The response, warm though it was, was disconcerting. There was no distinct location to attach it to—no mouth to see—and I wasn't even certain it was a voice in the ordinary sense. As I had briefly experienced with Norma and Sam, it could have been more like a thought appearing in my own mind.

"Are you pure light?" I asked.

The being chuckled. "I don't usually think of myself as pure. You could, however, say that I am only light. But realize," it went on with its authority, "that there are innumerable permutations and combinations of light. I am no more pure light than you yourself. Bodily projections are just that: projections and, like all projections, they are themselves light. Even when you were in your earthly existence and thought of yourself as having a body, it was still a projection. You were so attached to it, however, you thought of it as something solid when it was but an image."

I was not sure I understood. Nevertheless I was pleased. This person, whoever he or she was, did seem to be more in the know than Sam and Norma and more inclined to teach. To comprehend what it was saying, however, I needed to wrestle with its teachings at a less abstract level. "Do you have a bodily projection?" I inquired.

"Not at the moment, obviously," it answered, again with a chuckle. "I have the capacity to re-create one if you so desire, albeit only with considerable effort."

"I'd like that. Please show me if it's not too much trouble," I said with embarrassment.

Trouble though it might have been, it seemed effortless as a man immediately materialized before me. He was standing in the center of my little room, straight, tall, blond, and radiating health. He was wearing a plain gray tunic that looked to be made of a marvelously soft material. As with Sam and Norma, his body seemed to shimmer softly. I guessed his age to be thirty. There was something disturbingly familiar about him, but I couldn't quite put my finger on it, so I pushed it to the back of my mind. "How did you just do that?" I asked. "How did you materialize?"

"On one level it's simple," the man answered me. "I merely willed it. In that sense it's no different than the way you simply willed yourself back to earth yesterday."

"So you can read my mind too," I noted.

"Yes."

He spoke as if it was the most natural thing in the world, whereas for me it opened up a veritable Pandora's box of questions. I felt confused. I'd only started to explore the whole realm of bodily projections and now there was this whole new realm of mindreading. But my old training as a psychotherapist came to my aid. "When confused, take it slow—one little piece at a time," I had learned. So I returned to the issue of the body. "It was easy for me to go back to earth," I pointed out, "yet you said it would take you a lot of effort to will your body back."

"Let me try to explain," he volunteered. "All matter is a projection of spirit, but on earth no one understands that except a few theologians and physicists, and even then their understanding is purely theoretical. When we die there is a radical separation between our spirits and our bodily projections, but not quite a total divorce. The spirit becomes much stronger and its projections much weaker—so weak, in fact, that the people left back on earth can't see it anymore. That's why when you returned to earth yesterday they couldn't see you, could they?"

I acknowledged that was so. "But what about my corpse?" I interjected. "People could see that. They could even exhume me and dissect the smelly thing."

"Good point," my new mentor commented. "There are two things you need to realize. When I told you that all matter is a projection of spirit, that doesn't mean the projection isn't real. Matter exists. The other thing is that the only way I have to talk about it in this language is through analogy. When someone took a photograph of you, the print of that photograph was real in the sense that you could hold it, see it, feel it, even weigh it. But the photograph wasn't you, was it?"

"No. Just an image of me."

"And what would happen to that photograph over time?"

"It would yellow. Eventually turn to dust."

"Exactly. Ashes to ashes, dust to dust, like your corpse.

Your corpse is the material afterimage of you ... after you've left it."

I felt I vaguely understood, but only vaguely. This business of matter and spirit seemed like an unending intellectual quagmire from which I would never be able to fully extricate myself. The handsome man standing before me became a metaphorical tuft of seemingly solid earth in a bog, perhaps as much of a hindrance to my progress as a help. "But you're not a corpse," I argued in frustration.

"No, the image you see of me is very different. It is not material. You can best think of it as a meeting place of our wills—of my will to be seen by you and yours to see me. To use an analogy again, it's somewhat like a refraction pattern of light. Light is immaterial, yet when two beams of it collide it can leave visible traces. But remember that's just an analogy."

"Oh, shit," I muttered. Physics had never been my forte.

"Okay, forget about physics then," the being instructed, reading my mind again. "If you want out of the quagmire stop analyzing, and I won't have to use any more analogies. Suspend your disbelief and just listen to me for a few moments."

"I'll try," I said meekly.

"Souls on earth have material projections or bodies to which they are very attached. They can see others' bodies, but they have very little capacity to see immaterial projections. That's why they couldn't see you yesterday. Our souls, however, only have immaterial bodily projections. But these projections become weaker the longer we're here because our souls become less and less attached to the notion of having a body. When you first got here you thought a great deal about your body. Now a mere week into the Adjustment you're thinking relatively little about it. You may not realize it, but your projection has already become very weak. Mostly you look as I did when you first saw me, like a sort of ball of light, only with a vague sort of form about it." Here my mentor laughed. "In fact, you look for all the world like a ghost, quite fuzzy and transparent. But you can strengthen your projection simply by willing it. Go ahead. Try it."

I wished myself to appear clear and precise.

"Excellent!" my mentor exclaimed. "You look as solid as you did back on earth, and much as I imagined you might. Now relax. Just stop thinking about your body."

I did so.

The man laughed with pleasure. "It's really a shame we can't invent some kind of mirror that can capture immaterial projections. If you had such a mirror right now you could watch yourself fading away.

"A few more things," he went on. "If it takes you an act of will to demonstrate and maintain your immaterial bodily image after just a week here, think of how hard it is for me to do so after almost thirty years. Think also about the strength of will—of love—it must have taken Jesus to make his immaterial projection visible to human beings on earth after his crucifixion."

"That's what the Resurrection was about?"

"Of course. God knows what happened to his corpse. That's one of the stupid things about the Gospels. His corpse didn't get up and walk around. It was his soul that came back to earth and projected itself with such power that ordinary people could see him. So they would know he was still alive, that only the body dies . . . and only their bodies would die.

He was showing them his ghost, not his corpse. There the Gospels are accurate. It was obviously his ghost. Walking through the walls. Appearing and disappearing. Unrecognizable and then recognizable. Now you see him; now you don't."

I was exultant. For many years I'd secretly suspected this to be the nature of the Resurrection, but I was delighted to have it finally confirmed by an obvious authority. "Thank you," I said.

"Now can I too give up the ghost, so to speak?" my mentor asked with a smile.

"One more minute, please," I pleaded. "There's something familiar about you. I've been trying to think what it is. It just came to me. Although you're older, you remind me of my son, Timothy. He died when he was only seventeen."

My mentor smiled again. "It's not surprising I should remind you of him since I am he."

"You're Timmy?"

"Yes."

I knew it was so. Overwhelmed by feeling, I suddenly felt very shy. "I don't know what to do," I said haltingly. "I guess I'd most like to give you a hug."

"Go ahead," Timmy welcomed.

I did so, and nothing happened. There was nothing there, nothing to feel. I might as well have been embracing thin air. My face fell.

"I'm sorry, Dad," Timmy said. "Had I a body I'd be happy for you to hug it. But I also wanted to make it clear that it really is just a projection. Forgive me if it seems like a cheap trick."

"Me forgive you?" I responded. "Yes, it hurt for a second,

but reality's reality, isn't it? Even if you could project an image like Jesus did, I wouldn't have a finger to stick in your wounds or arms to hold you with. I'm the one who needs forgiveness, pushing you to keep up a bodily image when it takes work. Please let it go now."

Timmy instantly became his real bundle of light self again. "Thank you," he said. "It is much more relaxing."

I was still overwhelmed with feelings . . . and questions. The irony of the fact that my call for a highly sophisticated mentor was answered by my own son did not escape me. Yet it seemed perfectly appropriate. Timmy had always been an unusually sophisticated child, and by now he'd had almost thirty years' experience in this realm to my single week. I had no resistance to his being my teacher. Nevertheless a wave of fatherliness did flow over me. "Are you happy?" I asked.

"Of course," Timmy laughed. "I'm in heaven, aren't I?"

"Am I in heaven?" The question popped out, helpless as I was to inhibit my habitual desire for bearings.

"Yes. But as you're starting to realize, being in heaven is not bliss in the sense of unending emotional painlessness. The Adjustment has its pains, just as it hurt you a few moments ago to realize we couldn't physically hug . . . just as you've also experienced sadness and depression, confusion, doubt, and fear. And when you've completed the Adjustment, you'll continue to have painful feelings of one sort or another. But you will, in essence, be happy."

I started to tell him about Tish in her pink room down the corridor. I'd hardly begun when in that mindreading way of his—and of Norma and Sam—he jumped ahead of me. "You're right," he said, "she's in purgatory. It won't hurt for you to pray for her, but I doubt you have to worry about her very much. She'll be getting all the help she needs. That's what purgatory is all about—getting help—and she wouldn't be there unless she had the capacity to soften to it sooner or later."

I found myself able to fall easily into that rapidity of dialogue where I needed only to give a brief cue to what was on my mind. "And the trash can?" I asked.

"Yes, that's hell all right. You see, most mental disorders are psychosomatic," Timmy explained. "When a schizophrenic dies, because he's left his body behind he no longer has disordered brain chemicals to fight and he can think clearly again. But he'll likely go to purgatory because the Adjustment is so difficult. He has to get *used* to thinking clearly just as Tish has to get used to not being fat. Of course they need help and a bit of time before they can be in heaven. Other souls, however, have a far more serious illness which is purely spiritual. When they get here they're not like a Tish who's bored yet reluctant to listen to her Greeters; they're like cornered rats screaming for release. They can't stand the freedom here. They beg their Greeters to go to a place where they're endlessly busy fighting and evading the truth. They give the Greeters no choice except to refer them to Amalgamated Systems or its equivalent, and when they get there they dive in with relief."

The answers I wanted were coming in as fast as I could possibly receive them. Additional questions were popping up in my mind with equal rapidity. They were responded to, however, before I even had to ask. "No, it wasn't God's idea to put them in a trash can," Timmy continued. "It's their own. They're offered a room like this, and that's just for starters, but they flee it for the darkness. On a conscious level they'd like to have a huge office building, larger than anything else here, in order to assert their dominance, as so many of them had back on earth. But you see, things are real here. Their dwelling place is their projected image. Remember that professor at Harvard you told me about? The one who wanted to project an image of great importance but in reality came across to you merely as a pathetic name dropper? Consequently, the corporate image Amalgamated Systems projects despite itself is that of a garbage can. Sometimes I wonder if the poor souls way down deep think of themselves as garbage."

Many things touched me. It felt warm that Timmy had called me Dad. I was pleased he remembered the story I'd told him so many years ago back on earth about that Harvard professor. His reference to the souls at the bottom of the trash can as poor was not condescending but pregnant with empathy.

"Of course we don't just totally leave them alone," he went on before I had time to ask. "Let just one of them think, 'God, I'd like to get the hell out of here,' and a specially trained Greeter will be at his or her side in an instant. As well, we conduct an annual inspection of sorts where each soul is formally invited to meet with a Greeter. It's very rare they take us up. Still it happens that a soul who rejects us year after year may in a century or more literally see the light and come out with us."

"So all souls after their death exist here either in heaven, hell, or purgatory?" I concluded.

"That's virtually correct. There are only two extraordinarily infrequent exceptions," Timmy replied. "One is ghosts. They're souls who will not forsake their attachment to earth, usually because they won't give up some resentment. So they hang around ineffectually trying to haunt the place of their attachment. Basically they're in limbo. After a few hundred years they eventually get it into their head that they're ineffectual and getting nowhere so they finally give up and allow themselves to come here."

"And the other exception?"

"A dozen times or so in a generation a soul will be reincarnated from purgatory. Yes, there is such a thing as reincarnation. But it's not like people on earth tend to think. It's the exception, as I said, and not the rule. It's a very, very rare special case that only occurs when someone can't get out of purgatory through the ordinary means of healing. No, I'm not going to go into it any deeper, Dad. I know you were a psychiatrist and you've got an interest in such things. But you also know that each case is different and requires complex decisions. It's very technical, and if you want to explore it more fully I'm sure you can. You've got a world of time, you know."

I had to laugh at that and Timmy's awareness of my habitual impatience. But there was another technical area of which I had perhaps as much understanding as anyone on earth, which is to say extremely little. "What about angels and demons?" I asked.

"Pretty much as you've guessed from the combination of mythology and your experience. God created the angels before human beings. Even before many of the animals. He created them to be his helpers in overseeing evolution. They're semi-autonomous and have something like souls. You might think of them as proto-souls—a very early model, so to speak. When God created humans as an improved model to eventually be better than the angels, Satan rebelled, and with the minions he took with him, has been trying to destroy humanity ever since. And they keep at it even though it's obviously a losing battle. That's the way it is with angels, dark or light; they're not very smart, you know. Oh, in some ways they're smarter than most humans, but they don't begin to match humans at their best. They don't have the same degree of freedom of will, so they don't have the potential flexibility. They're a bit robot-like. They're incomplete spirits. That's another way to think of them: as isolated archetypes. They can be very powerful in their own limited sphere. A living archetype can be an awesome thing to behold, but it's still limited like a kind of idiot savant."

Timmy was correct. It was pretty much as I had guessed. But it was good to have my guesses confirmed, not that I still didn't have a thousand questions. Nevertheless they were what he would properly call technical questions, and I had an eternity to search for the answers if I wanted. Besides, even I was becoming uneasy on this intellectual plane. There were some far more personal questions I needed to ask, and I suspected I'd been putting them off precisely because they were personal. It's easier to speak of the intellectual than the intimate. "Timmy," I began, "do you know why you died so young?"

"On the surface. I was what my friends used to call 'an old soul,' as if I'd been born somehow already knowing most of the lessons life on earth has to teach. Why I was an old soul I don't know except it had nothing to do with reincarnation. Maybe it had to do with my genes. Both you and Mom had a bit of an old soul, whether you were aware of it or not. Nor do I know why it was specifically leukemia or why it was at seventeen instead of twelve or twenty-five. But being born with an old soul is a bit like being born tired. I really didn't want to live very much. It had nothing to do with you and Mom. The two of you treated me very well. Almost too well. It was just that I was always yearning to come here."

It was what we'd suspected, I told him. "In fact, we'd had premonitions you might die young long before the leukemia, but we never shared them with you lest it seem we wanted you to die."

"I sort of wish you had shared them," Timmy responded, "since I had them myself. It would have made me feel less lonely and peculiar. I don't think I would have felt less loved. But you're correct it might have encouraged me to die all the earlier. Yet I am also grateful that at the end you allowed me to refuse that last chemo and you told me you were ready to let me go if that was what I wanted and how I shouldn't feel guilty for leaving you. That really helped."

"You said your mother and I treated you almost too well," I commented. "Could you say more?"

"It's just a vague feeling. You were generally so nice and thoughtful and accommodating and liberal, I felt I didn't have any right to get angry at you. There was practically nothing for me to rebel against. Maybe it would have made me feel less guilty had you given me some tough love."

"Are there some other things I need to be forgiven for?"

Timmy chuckled. "Yes, that time when I was eight and you wouldn't let me go to Europe alone."

"Well, there was a bit of tough love." I laughed. "I'm not sure the State Department would have let you go either." I paused for a moment. "Timmy, have you seen your mother?"

"A couple of times."

"Is she well?"

"Why, of course. She's in heaven too, you know."

"Do you think she'll want to see me?" I asked.

"I can't say for sure, but I don't see why not. I heard you guys had it pretty good at the end."

"Yes, we had it pretty good. Any suggestions how I should approach her?"

"Well, you could call for her and she'd probably come here just as I did. But somehow I think she'd rather you came to her. Wish and see what happens. You'll either get to her or else, if she doesn't want to see you, nothing will happen."

That seemed simple enough, although it hardly relieved me of all my anxiety. I switched the subject. "What do you do here, Timmy?"

"You'll find out pretty soon, I imagine. A lot of committee work mostly. It's fun."

Sam and Norma had mentioned committees. Now Timmy. But he'd done so in such a way as to clearly indicate he didn't want to get into details. Not for the moment at least. So I switched the subject again. "I asked for a mentor to come to me. I didn't expect it to be you, but I couldn't have chosen better. Efficient. Killed two birds with one stone," I noted. "I wanted to see you in the first place and you've been a perfect mentor in the second."

"I know."

"But how did you know? You came instantly. Were you just sitting around waiting for me to call?"

"Yes and no. I knew you'd finally come here. I knew I'd be a good mentor for starters. And I wanted to see you too,

Dad. But, no, I wasn't quite sitting around. I was in a committee meeting when your call came."

"So you interrupted your work to come to me? Am I so important or is it so unimportant?"

"Neither," my son said with what felt to me to be a grin. "Or both. You remember yesterday when you were visiting Tintagel you discovered you could go back and forth in time?"

"Yes."

"Well, we can do that here too. As soon as I leave here I'll go back in time and return to the meeting right at the point that I left it when I got your call. I won't have missed a thing. And the committee won't have missed me."

"No kidding?" I was a bit dumbstruck.

"Or I could have done it the other way around," Timmy added. "I could have stayed at the meeting until its conclusion and then gone back in time so as to arrive here right when you called. But I was curious about you. I didn't want to sit around at the meeting wondering how you were doing. It might have distracted me."

"So you can bilocate," I said with awe.

"Sure. I suppose I could trilocate . . . or quadrilocate for that matter . . . but I've never had the occasion to want to. It's no big deal. Anyone here can do it. You can do it."

"I've heard some reports of Hindu gurus doing it back on earth," I commented.

"Yeah. Frankly, I don't know whether they're true or not. Maybe the reports are apocryphal."

"Aren't you curious?" I asked.

"Not particularly."

Although he seemed much more knowledgeable than Sam

and Norma, I suddenly felt in Timmy their same, almost bland, lack of curiosity. Did the afterlife somehow blunt one's taste for inquiry, I wondered? As it seemed to have blunted mine yesterday? But only partially blunted! Maybe I wasn't going to get any further with Hindu gurus, but there were other avenues I was desperate to explore. "When you were sitting in that meeting, how did you get my call?" I asked. "In fact, how are we communicating at all? Right here without mouths or ears? I know you're going to tell me it's some kind of telepathy, but how does it work?" I was desperate. "How does it work?" I repeated.

"I don't know."

"You don't know?"

"No. I'm not going to be able to satisfy you, Dad."

"Can't you at least try? Please," I pleaded.

"Remember back when we were talking about will and material projections and spiritual projections, and I used the analogy of light?"

"Yes."

"What is light, Dad?"

The tables had been turned. "I don't know," I had to admit. "And as far as I can understand it, even the most advanced nuclear physicists don't know. They'll tell you it's energy, but that doesn't seem to explain anything because they don't really seem to understand the essence of energy."

"Do you think they ever will understand?"

I could guess where Timmy was going. In the Middle Ages—the Age of Faith—people pretty much took light for granted. In the seventeenth century they seriously began to study it. The Age of Reason had dawned. By the eighteenth century they thought they almost had it all figured out. In the nineteenth they began to increasingly argue about it. And in the twentieth they became more and more confused.

"No," I acknowledged. "I doubt that they ever will understand it. The deeper they go, the closer they get, the more elusive it seems to become. I guess it's sort of like God."

"Sort of?" Timmy echoed.

I was silent.

"Let's say that all these things are synonyms," he continued. "Light. Energy. Will. God. And why don't I throw in consciousness while I'm at it? And let's just say that God is the source of them all . . . in fact, *is* them in their essence. Their purity. Then all is a manifestation of God. Not so much a reflection, like a photograph—an image I used before—but simply superficial. Superficial, like surface. Then we—you and I, our wills, our thoughts, our energy of communication—are all the surface of God. Not to denigrate us. A surface can be the cutting edge of the essence. That's dignified, isn't it? Maybe you and I, and our communication at this very moment, are the cutting edge of God. On the other hand," here Timmy laughed, "the notion that we are God can be considered a figure of speech . . . so to speak."

So I was back in the quagmire with nothing more to grab hold of than the vague and paradoxical concepts that mystics back on earth had been mouthing for millennia. My first instinct was to be irritated with Timmy. But then this matter of light grabbed hold of *me.* On earth I had taken delight in the fact that the best minds were at a loss when it came to wrapping light—and other things—into a nice, neat, little package that they could put in their intellectual briefcases. I reveled that the mystery of the world was larger than them.

Yet now I found the same mystery annoying. I began to laugh at myself.

"I think I've spotted a false assumption," I said. "I used to be comfortable—happy even—that not all things were explainable. But part of my comfort was the hope that when I died all things would be revealed. I somehow assumed that there would be no mystery in heaven. But I guess that's not true, is it?"

"Congratulations!" Timmy exclaimed. "You've got it! What you assumed was a lack of curiosity on my part and in your Greeters is simply a knowledge of our limitations. You will grow closer to God here. Yet at the same time God will remain wonderfully mysterious. You wouldn't have it otherwise, would you? Would you really like to live in a world where there was no mystery left?"

"I guess not," I answered with a hint of dubiousness. Still, I was awed by Timmy's mirthful tranquility. "When I called you," I went on, "I was calling for a mentor. And you have been that. But I have a sense I'm going to need a good deal more instruction. Would you continue to be my mentor?"

"No," Timmy replied, but the rejection felt not only gentle but almost uplifting. "It's not that we're related. It would be an honor for a son to be a mentor to his father. And you have honored me, Dad. But other mentors will be coming to you—ones that are more appropriate in the order of things."

"What order is that?"

Timmy laughed. "Always in a hurry, aren't you, Dad? You'll find out. Soon. Soon enough. Don't worry. Just wait a little bit."

"I've never been good at waiting."

"No, you haven't. Speaking of which, I think it's about time I get back to my meeting."

Anxiety clutched me. "Will I see you again?" I blurted. "Can I see you again?"

"Sure. If you need to. Or if I need to see you. But don't be surprised if we find that there's no need."

We were clearly saying our goodbyes, but I had to hang on for a moment. "Is there any one thing you can tell me before you leave?" I pleaded. "One word of advice?"

"Yes. Relax. Lighten up, Dad. A lot of your questioning isn't just curiosity; it's a way of intellectually trying to get an ultimately sterile and impossible kind of control over things. Jesus said we must be as wise as serpents and innocent as doves. You don't have to throw out your wisdom, your intellect. It's God-given. But you might strengthen your innocence some. You're safe here, you know. This is a safe place."

"I love you, Timmy," was all I could say.

"I love you, too, Daddy," he responded, and then he was gone.

He was right about my need to lighten up. And the genesis of the problem. At the deepest level of my being I was ruled by a sense that the world was *not* a safe place—a sense that things would get dangerously out of control unless I stayed rigorously on top of them. It was my old Daniel complex, of course. Much as I tried to remind myself that there was obviously no lions' den here, I remained, for the moment, a man of little faith. It was not all bad. My often excessive alertness had saved the day on a number of occasions back on earth. " 'Twas grace that taught my heart to fear . . .

as well as grace my fears relieved." But what I needed now was the fear-relieving kind of grace, the grace of innocent faith in my safety and the safety of those I loved.

I prayed for that grace. As I did my mind gradually drifted off to Mary Martha. Meeting Timmy had made me all the more eager to see her again. I wanted to share my delight in him. But what if she didn't want to see me? What if she rejected me? What if our meeting didn't go well? What if . . .

CHAPTER

9

T oday was Mary Martha day! I was excited as a schoolboy. And as terrified.

My fear that she might reject me was not merely my Daniel complex. Even more it was a matter of boundaries. Mary Martha and I were strong-willed people, each in our own way powerful. Much of the first half of our marriage we'd spent trying to win, me trying to win her over to my way of thinking and she attempting to tame me to hers. We waged the struggle ever so politely, but it was a losing battle for both of us.

So gradually we learned how to make peace through the establishment of proper boundaries. We learned how to give each other space. It wasn't easy. One of the prices we had to pay was that of celibacy during the latter half of our marriage. As long as we looked to each other for sex, our separate spaces would get all mixed up and needs to dominate would resurface.

I was so eager so see Mary Martha again, therefore, not for

any sexual reason. Even if sex was possible here without a body, my libido had been negligible in my latter years when I did have a body, and it had not been directed at her for years before that. As far as I was concerned, I had outgrown sex and was glad of it. In my younger days my sexual passions were so powerful they'd often seemed more like a curse than a blessing—a curse I thought I was quite content to leave in the past.

Nor was my deep desire to see Mary Martha a romantic one in the ordinary sense. Romance is largely a matter of illusion, and whatever illusions we once had harbored in relationship to each other had long ago evaporated. Indeed, the beauty of our marriage in its last two decades was its reality. We saw each other clearly: our strengths and weaknesses, capacities and limitations, virtues and vices. More importantly, we accepted all that we saw. We had become utterly acceptable in each other's eyes. Although not as thrilling as romance, it was something better. It was, in fact, true love.

So I wanted to see Mary Martha on this morning because I loved her as much as myself. I loved her almost as much as I loved God. So too had she loved me. But that was three years ago, and I had no idea what changes she might have undergone since. We had needed boundaries and, for all I knew, today she might need them still more. There was no guarantee she'd want me in her space at all. "Sweetheart," I prayed to her, "you have no obligation to me, but I dearly want to come to you if you'll have me."

My heart leaped. Mary Martha was standing before me looking exactly as I remembered: wearing the brown-checked tweed coat that made her seem just about ready to ride to the hounds despite the fact she loved foxes and hated riding the gentlest horse; her short, cropped gray hair with its usual touch of wildness that in no way detracted from her dignity; her thick waist she always assumed I despised no matter how perfectly honest my protestations to the contrary; the twinkle of mischief in her eyes that consistently caused her to look a good ten years younger. "You're lovely," I exclaimed. "And just the same."

"You're not," she retorted. "You look distinctly indistinct."

I realized Mary Martha, with her customary thoughtfulness, had projected her bodily image to welcome me while I'd given no thought to my own appearance. I consciously projected my image.

"You haven't changed either," Mary Martha responded. "Still the same mixture of old man and little boy."

By this time I'd become aware of the room. It was huge in comparison to mine and as elegant as mine was drab. The basic color was a very light gray—walls, ceiling, and thick carpet—that only served to augment the riot of primary colors; huge vases of fresh flowers on polished tables; a sofa and chair set that was bright orange without being the slightest bit gaudy; three modern impressionist paintings that perfectly captured the kind of green coasts we'd so loved in northern Spain. "You've made yourself a gorgeous home," I commented, "although I shouldn't be surprised. You've always created beautiful homes for us, and as usual you've surrounded yourself with flowers."

"Thank you," Mary Martha acknowledged. "It's good to see you again. But are you aware that you're already starting to fade once more?"

"I'm sorry," I apologized. "I met Timmy yesterday, and he told me how difficult it was for him to project a bodily image.

Now I understand. It's something that takes conscious effort. As soon as I started becoming aware of how lovely this room is, I forgot about my image. But then I always did have trouble being conscious of two things simultaneously."

"That's true," Mary Martha teased.

"I never knew which one of us was normal," I said. "As you remember, I used to think it was bizarre how you could hold an intense, important business conversation on the phone while playing a computer game at the same time. But right now it seems to give you a rather obvious competitive advantage."

"Who's competing?"

"It was just a figure of speech," I protested.

She decided to let me get away with it. "Actually," she admitted, "it does tire me to maintain these images for long."

I failed to pick up on her use of the plural. "It's been a gift for me to see you again," I told her. "But now I have, it would be quite all right with me if we were to stop keeping up appearances."

I hadn't fully bargained for what came next. "Okay," Mary Martha said and instantly there was nothing. She was gone and the gorgeous room was gone. All was dark gray, as if we were in a fog so dense you could not see your own hand. I had been plunged into nothingness. Terror came over me. It seemed I no longer existed. Nothing existed.

"Don't be afraid."

It was Mary Martha's voice. Or something like her voice. My terror began to subside as I realized that this was not quite nothingness. For one thing, I was still conscious. I was conscious of my terror and of its waning. For another, Mary Martha continued to exist. Although I could not see it, I could sense her presence close to me—so close it was almost as if she was cradling me. "Where are we?" I cried.

"In a place where the day and night, the light and dark, have not been separated."

"Like before creation?"

"Exactly."

"But we're still conscious?"

"Of course, silly. We're communicating, aren't we?" I could almost hear Mary Martha giggling at me.

"So consciousness precedes creation?"

The giggle seemed to become louder. "Always a theologian, aren't you, Danny? Always trying to get God pinned down and put in His place."

I acknowledged this to be the case, but was hardly about to be deterred. "Because we're conscious in a place as if it preceded creation, does that mean we're gods?" I asked.

"Sort of. In a way. But don't ask me to go deeper."

So I was going to be deterred, as least as far as this line of inquiry was concerned. Mary Martha had indicated she didn't want to go deeper. I knew the strength of her will. She meant what she said. I switched tracks. "I've become accustomed to seeing souls here as a kind of light," I commented. "I'm surprised now that I can't see your light."

"There's nothing to see it by," she explained. "Light needs structure to become visible. Were we back in the structure of my room, or your little green room, you'd see my light. It's not much different than back on earth, you know. You can't generally see light except when it hits an object or at least has a structure to be contrasted against."

I understood . . . more or less. But the explanation opened up a whole other area for questions. My little green room was there whenever I was. It didn't just vanish the way her elegant one had.

As had Timmy and my Greeters, Mary Martha was now reading my mind and had begun answering my questions before I asked them. "Consciousness here creates appearances," she instructed. "When you came to my room I wasn't attending to two things at once but three: to you, to my appearance or projected image, and to the image of the room. When you suggested we stop keeping up appearances, naturally not only did I disappear but also the room and the structure by which I could see your light, or by which you could see mine.

"And now you're wondering why your little green room doesn't disappear too," she continued. "That's because others are thinking about it even when you're not. You could say they are praying it into existence around the clock."

"But why?"

"What would it have been like for you if you had immediately come to this nothingness?"

Just imagining it brought back a taste of the terror I'd felt only a few moments ago. Then I recalled that Norma and Sam had already explained the reason for my little green room. How was it I'd forgotten? As then, a sense of gratitude poured over me that others—or God—had gone to so much trouble to prepare a place for me. In fact, I now realized, they were still doing so. But how does one live with constant gratitude? I was not nearly ready for heaven, it seemed. My all too human tendency was to quickly take such caring for granted and forget. Just as I had taken the verdancy of earth for granted.

"Do you remember, darling," I remarked, "how I used to

poke fun at those philosophers who concluded that nothing on earth existed unless it was being thought of? How they claimed maybe a tree never fell in the forest if there was no one to hear it fall? I thought they were so ridiculous. I'd joke about how when I stubbed my toe against a chair in the dark, it wasn't because I was thinking that chair into existence; I was stubbing my toe precisely because I wasn't thinking about it. Now it occurs to me I was being self-centered. Although I wasn't thinking about the chair, maybe somebody up here was thinking about it."

"No, you were right," Mary Martha responded. "The world of the flesh is not an illusion. Regardless of how it might have originally been created, it mostly exists independently of us here. We don't have to go around thinking of daffodils all the time for there to be daffodils on earth. Or armadillos. Matter is real. So is spirit. But just because spirit is real—and ultimately more important—it doesn't mean that matter isn't really matter."

"Regardless of how the world might have been originally created," I repeated. "Do you know how it was created?"

The answer was stark. "No."

I was reminded of how Timmy teased me about my silly expectation that somehow there'd be no mystery left in heaven. "So you can't prove the Big Bang Theory for me," I chided.

"No, but I can tell you that as far as earth is concerned, there's much more to it than that. It's much sexier."

"Sexier?"

"Yes, metaphorically, but I don't feel up to saying more at the moment."

The boundary was clear again. I fell silent, and soon was

glad of it, for in the silence I felt Mary Martha's presence more acutely. With thought pushed aside for a moment, there was a lovely sense of peace between us. It reminded me of those moments after the two of us had had sex together and were lying next to each other in the darkness somewhere in between physical depletion and the full resumption of thought. It was not a sexual feeling exactly, but in this place of emptiness I experienced us as powerfully intimate.

Out of the intimacy Mary Martha softly asked, "Was it hard for you to die, Danny? Leave your body, I mean? My death was so sudden, I didn't even know it. No suffering at all. But you had cancer. What was it like?"

"Not bad at all. They gave me all the pain medicine I needed, and at the end I was in coma. With you gone, I had no real desire to live. I suppose it would have been horrible otherwise."

"Are you sure you're not just playing the man and making light of it?"

"Well, I was giving you the bright side, I guess," I admitted. "But you know a good deal about the dark side. Remember how we used to moan and groan together about our aging—how it seemed to be a stripping away of everything? My cancer was simply more of it, as if it speeded up the aging process. There was something frightening . . . dreadful . . . full of dread . . . in watching my body waste away daily. Yet I fancied I needed the experience, that my death was slower than yours perhaps because I needed more stripping than you did."

In the silence that followed I pondered the strange, paradoxical nature of my relationship to my body . . . and to bodies. Mostly I'd disliked my body, not because I'd thought it ugly but because I'd seen it as the source of so much pain: of colds and fevers and flu, of backaches and fatigue, of surgery for this and surgery for that. At the same time, I'd clung to it, as if there was some force in each of its cells shrieking, "Keep me alive, keep me alive!" Much as I'd wanted to discard my body, my dying process had been wrenching.

I also thought of sex, of the beauty of a woman's breasts and thighs, a beauty that was more than beauty, that was strangely akin to glory. And of the ecstasy of orgasm. Was that ecstasy a blessing *of* the body or a blessing of liberation *from* the body? Who knew? I had no sense of missing it that I was aware of but I couldn't help remember. God, how I had loved sex in my day!

All that was a long time ago, however, and now I was perfectly content with bodiless intimacy. "Since I've grown a bit accustomed to it," I commented, "I'm feeling remarkably peaceful in the midst of this nothingness, at least as long as I can sense your presence beside me."

"When I leave, you can always return to your little green room, you know," Mary Martha reassured me.

"Yes, I've been assuming that to be the case. What's surprising me at the moment is not so much my peacefulness as yours," I told her. "You weren't always so on earth. We both desperately needed our nests, but of the two of us you seemed the one more attached to particular things: to clothes, to furniture, to little decorations and mementos."

"You're right," she acknowledged with ease. "My Adjustment was relatively simple, to my own surprise. What I quickly discovered, however, was that my attachment to things was mostly one to *playing* with things. You remember how much I loved to rearrange the furniture from time to time?"

"Indeed."

"When I first came here I had my own little green room—only it was beige. It was boring until I gradually realized I could furnish it in my imagination. If I wished or prayed hard enough, anything I wanted would appear: an eighth-century mosaic, a Swedish modern desk, whatever silver place-setting I desired, a particular Rembrandt or Renoir. Only they all vanished as soon as I stopped thinking about them. At first that discouraged me, but as soon as I became involved in other things, I came to delight in the change-ability of it all.

"You see, whenever I need to sleep or relax, I can nest here in the nothingness with complete comfort. I know I'm safe. But if I get bored I can temporarily create a room and decorate it just as I did for you. That was fun. And it was fun showing it off to you, just as I used to do. I may create the exact same room next time. It *was* good. Or I might do it just a little bit differently. Or else do something totally different. We could have met in a Gothic cathedral with stained glass windows had I wanted it. It's wonderful."

Her delight was almost palpable, and I rejoiced in it. And in her. She was very much the same Mary Martha with the same earthy and girlish excitement over little things that I'd so loved about her. But I too was excited to share things. I told her how well her gardens were being maintained. I recounted Timmy's mentorship of me the day before and my brief observations of Vicky and Marshall on earth the day before that . . . if days they were. Mary Martha listened, but to my surprise when I was finished she expressed no further interest. "Don't you want to know more?" I asked.

"Not particularly."

"But . . ."

"I could tell you about my own, quite similar visits with them." Mary Martha silenced my astonishment. "You're correct, however, in picking up on my relative disinterest. If they were doing badly, I'd be concerned, of course. I'd quickly go into prayer. But they're doing well. You may not remember it but, like you, I'd also begun to emotionally separate from the children in my later years. Still, not as much as you, and when I first got here I thought it would be a big problem. To my amazement, it wasn't. I was surprised at how rapidly and naturally I became detached. I used to laugh because I sometimes found myself starting to think like you: coldly rational and objective yet fascinated by the big picture in certain ways. My God, am I turning into Daniel? I wondered. Yes, if you asked me the biggest way in which I've changed, I'd have to answer that I've become much more detached."

So she was and wasn't the same old Mary Martha.

"You mentioned you've become involved in other things," I inquired. "Like what?"

"Committee work mostly."

Committees again! Sam and Norma had told me they'd been selected and trained as Greeters by some sort of committee. I'd called Timmy out of a committee. Perhaps it was a committee that was praying my little green room into existence. And now Mary Martha. "Does everyone in heaven work in committees?" I asked.

"Naturally. And it's lovely, darling. The committees here—heaven, that is—all work according to the principles of community. Many of them are the same principles that you more or less discovered back on earth." Here Mary Martha giggled. "Were you aware twenty-five years ago that you were discovering principles of heavenly operations?"

"You were helping me," I reminded her. "But no, I wasn't aware of it. I did know the whole business had something to do with God, of course, and I did see the rules of community building as being the laws for creating a miracle of sorts. Still, I was never thinking of heaven. I was just trying to discern how groups of people could work together most successfully on earth."

"Only here they work even better!" Mary Martha exclaimed with joy, beginning to roll. "It's like we're in community all the time. We almost never fall out of it. We pick up on it as soon as there's any tension and just go deeper in prayer, praying our tensions into the light. Of course there are reasons it works so well, so much more easily than back on earth. Nobody's got any hidden agendas here. In fact, most of the time no one's got a personal agenda at all. And then there's the training. I can hardly wait for you to see it. It's done so much better than we used to do it. Inevitably. Everyone's got time here, all the time in the world, so everybody gets gobs of training. I guess you could say that by the time we get to work everybody's become an adult."

"And what is your work?" I asked when she finally came to a pause.

She rolled on. "My work? You need to realize there are millions of committees. My particular committee focuses on the creation of souls. Not all souls. Just a few. It takes a lot of work to create a soul, you know. There's work to be done before conception, prenatal work, and postnatal work, and it's all individualized, of course. So my committee is just one of thousands upon thousands of similar committees. Then there are even more committees in charge of nurturing souls, and sometimes we committees need to work hand in hand. The creation of souls is sometimes inseparable from their nurturance."

"I can understand that," I said. "But how do you create a soul?"

"Didn't I tell you it takes a lot of work? You expect me to tell you almost everything I've learned these past three years? No way. You'll find out in time. But it will take time. I'm not trying to put you off unfairly. I'm in the same position you were so often back on earth whenever you lectured on community building and you'd have to disappoint your audiences by telling them it wasn't something that could be learned from a lecture. You'd always give them the analogy of computers, remember? You'd explain how you couldn't learn about computers by reading a book about them, much less by listening to a single lecture; that people can only learn about computers by *doing* them, which takes a lot of time and effort. Oh, Danny, I could tell you how to create souls if we sat down for several months doing it together, but even then you'd only have the rudiments. Besides, there are much more efficient ways for each of us to use our time."

Mary Martha may not have wanted to put me off unnecessarily, but I was *feeling* put off. She was quite correct that I'd put off many thousands of people in exactly the same way for exactly the same reason. But I didn't like being one of them. I was coming to accept that there could be—even should be—mystery in heaven as there was on earth. What I found it harder to accept was that there were *answers* in

143

heaven that I was simply going to have to wait to learn. Waiting had never exactly been my strong suit. Particularly when it came to answers I knew were already there. It suddenly struck me that on the level of inquiry I functioned much as an emotional two-year-old.

Another area of inquiry occurred to me. It seemed potentially critical of Mary Martha's work. Was the criticism implied hostile? Motivated by my annoyance at being put off by her? By a competitiveness aroused by the clearly stated fact she possessed a knowledge that I did not? I didn't know. But when I emptied myself as best I could of my competitiveness and annoyance and impatience, the question was still left hanging in the air. So I asked it.

"You've made it clear that there's a great deal of work involved in the creation of even a single human soul," I said. "By the fact you do it in committees submitted to the principles of community, prayerfully, I assume you do that work with enormous care. You create souls with love. Only that leaves me with a question that may seem a criticism. How is it that such work often seems unsuccessful? Why doesn't it work out? Why do a few human beings, to all appearances, seem to be born without souls? You remember how when I was practicing psychotherapy I used to agonize over such rare cases, people who seemed literally empty underneath their flesh. More commonly, how is it that souls created in love seem to turn out actively malignant? And that millions end up in the kind of garbage can that's down the corridor from my little green room?"

"You're surprised that we often fail?" There was no hint of discomfort in Mary Martha's tone, only a touch of irony.

"Frankly, yes."

144

"Even though as a scientist you were quite familiar with failed experiments?"

"We're talking about the creation of souls," I protested. "We're not talking about some kind of experiment."

"Oh, but we are," Mary Martha announced definitively. "The creation of each and every individual soul is an experiment."

"An experiment?"

"Of course. Each soul is brand new. We have some guidelines we've learned to go by, needless to say, but they're only guidelines. It's a new creation, essentially a new experiment, each and every time. We don't *know* how it will turn out. All we've got is our best guesses. You're right: we make those guesses with love. It's not remarkable that many of them are wrong. What's wonderful is that so many of them are right, and that we seem to succeed a bit more often than we fail."

I'm not sure why I was astonished, but it was still taking me time to come to terms with the idea. All I could do was dumbly echo once more, "An experiment?"

"Yes, and always full of surprises. Take animals—dogs, for instance—as a simple example. We don't spend on them anything like the attention we spend on human souls, because dogs are an old experiment and humans a new one. So the souls of dogs are created pretty much by formula. But every great once in a while a dog will appear with a particularly unique and lovely soul, as if it managed to do the formula one better. Then we pay a lot of attention—not only from one of the committees on soul nurturance but also one of our committees on soul creation. We want to study the phenomenon to see if we can discern how and why that particular dog was such a success. And, as you might imagine, we pay equally great attention to our most striking failures, such as our Hitlers. Naturally, we work hard not only on each new human soul but also on the whole experimental design: the grand design of evolution, if you will. It can always be improved upon."

"So evolution doesn't just happen?"

"It plods along by itself much of the time. But we do interfere ever so gently now and then and give it a little boost. You know that, silly. I don't know why you're playing stupid. You even wrote about it thirty years ago."

"I wrote about God somehow inputting into it, yes. Are you saying that you're God?"

This time she seemed willing to go a little deeper into the subject. "No more than you are. Each of us is a tiny, tiny piece of God . . . in a sense. Only in a sense. But, yes, you could say that in our committees we are doing some of the work of God."

I felt strangely anxious. I could have asked Mary Martha at this point if she had met God. Had seen God. Had talked with God. But I knew full well that this business of meeting, seeing, or talking was all a matter of metaphor. I knew in the language we were using—and that itself was a metaphor since we were not actually speaking as we nestled together in this void—we were bogged down by mental models. Hypothetical constructs of reality, but not the reality itself, and certainly not the reality of God. At least I was bogged down. My anxiety was that of a man who suddenly realized he had stumbled upon holy ground.

"You're correct," Mary Martha said, reading my mind. "There's no way we can do God justice. But know this: all creation is an experiment. Not just the creation of a soul. All creation. It is God's experiment. Things can always go wrong. God is not a mere mathematician or accountant or even a lawmaker. God can be a lawbreaker too. God is a creator, an artist. But it's a good experiment. It would be changed if it wasn't. Meanwhile the results are beneficial on the whole. Remember the first chapter of Genesis: that God did this and saw that it was good, so He went on to do some more, and when He saw that that was good too, He went still further. That's the way it was, and that's the way it still is now. And that's all I've got to say on the subject for the moment. I'm tired."

I understood how she was tired. On earth one of my visions of the afterlife was that it might be a place where no one got tired anymore. Now I could laugh at my naiveté. Mary Martha had repeatedly referred to the soul-creating activity of her committee as work. Of course. It only made sense that there would be work to be done in heaven, and as much as it might also be like a kind of play it was naturally tiring. These conversations were the work of my adjustment . . . and the work of others helping me with it. Indeed, conversations was not the right word for them; they were too intense. Whatever the mechanics of communication and experience, whether here in the void or in my little green room, these teachings took energy of a sort and were depleting. I too was tired.

Yet there was a piece of unfinished business. Much could wait, but not this. "What about us?" I asked. "Back on earth we knew full well, as Jesus taught, that there'd be no marriage in heaven. Still, here we are relating, and while it's been tiring, for me it's also been exhilarating. It's been very

147

good to see you again, and I've found myself loving you just as I used to. To me it still feels like a vibrant relationship. It may not be marriage, and I don't want to have any hooks in you, but it doesn't feel right to me that I'll never see you again."

"Nor to me," Mary Martha responded. "I was just as curious as you about this meeting. I didn't know how I'd feel after three years. But you're right. Whether you call it love or magic, we still do seem to have something special going for us. I've no need to make plans, but I don't know why we shouldn't meet again sometime if and when the spirit moves us both. This may be heaven, and I've met a lot of good souls here, yet none I care for more. You're a good soul, Danny."

"Do they have vacations here?" I asked.

"What a lovely idea!" Mary Martha exclaimed. I could sense her sparkling the way she used to whenever we began to plot one of our trips. "I've been enjoying my work so much that I hadn't even thought about it. But, yes, there's no reason we couldn't go off on a holiday sometime."

"We always did travel well together," I commented.

"True. Let me know when you've settled in at your own work."

"I will."

"Right now I need to check in at mine before I have a nap."

"Go to it," I said.

And she did. I sensed her presence vanish. I chose not to return to my little green room right away so that I might experience what it was like to be in the void alone.

At first it was most pleasant. I was feeling warm and content and a bit high, almost as if I'd just had a shot of morphine. And for good reason. The meeting with Mary Martha was all I'd hoped for. It wasn't that I had to have everything stable. It wasn't even that we would see each other again soon; it might be close to an eon. It was simply that I'd not wanted to see a good thing die unnecessarily. In meeting with her I was prepared to face the possibility our relationship had died. But it hadn't. Apparently still vibrant things did not have to die in heaven. Maybe that was one definition of heaven: a place where still vibrant things were not terminated.

After a while my sense of fatigue began to return. I gave thought to simply going to sleep there in the void, and realized I could do so with relative ease; it was not beyond me. Nevertheless returning to my little green room felt like the greater ease. I pondered this. The key, it seemed to me, lay in the concept "my." Although not inherently unpleasant, the void was utterly anonymous. Any soul could inhabit it. It belonged to no one. My little green room, however, had specifically been prepared for me. For the moment. For the moment, it was mine. The phenomenon, I realized, was one of ego. There was something rather silly about preferring to sleep in a place that was mine as opposed to a place equally comfortable. For the moment, however, there didn't seem to be any need to call the question.

So I wished—prayed—myself back into my little green room. It did not seem wicked to pay such homage to my ego for a little while longer. After all, Rome was not built in a day, was it?

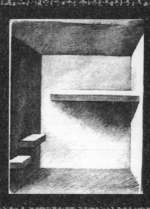

CHAPTER

10

After sleep I prayed for my Greeters. It was almost no time before Sam and Norma made their appearance in my little green room. "Wearing" their bodily projections, they looked exactly as I'd remembered them. "Thanks for coming," I welcomed them. "By the way, I've learned how much energy it takes to show up in body form. Please feel free to be however you like."

Instantly the two dematerialized into balls of light. No, not balls—the circumferences were too vague and fuzzy. Not even bundles of light. Foci was the best word that came to mind. Each was a separate, indistinct, yet definite focus of light. Although their lights looked much the same, they *felt* very different. I could feel Norma's motherly femininity and Sam's masculine nature. The lights had personalities. Indeed, I could somehow sense each of their personalities more clearly than if they had been in bodily form.

"You're all light!" Sam exclaimed. "Not a trace of your

body left. The Adjustment must be going well for you."

"I told you he'd be a fast mover," Norma reminded.

"Sometimes I move too fast for my own good," I commented. "My impatience tends to drive me. And if I'm doing well, you deserve a lot of the credit. That's one of the two reasons I asked to see you: to thank you."

"For what?" Sam asked.

"When you greeted me I was frightened and confused. Everything was so new. All the rules seemed to have changed. You made me feel much more solid, so to speak. Safe. You kept telling me how ordinary you were, but it was only after you'd left that it dawned on me that you'd greeted me with extraordinary skill. So thank you very much."

"Aw, you don't have to thank us," Sam responded. "We are ordinary. It's just that we've gotten some good training."

"Samuel, Samuel," Norma sighed with exasperation. "Why can't you take credit for something just once in your life? We are good at what we do, you know." There was a pause. Then she asked, "You said there were two reasons you wanted to see us. What's the other one?"

"To find out what's next," I answered. I quickly explained all that had happened to me since I'd last seen them: my visit to Tish in her pink purgatory; the experience with the hell of Amalgamated Systems; my return to earth; the reunion with Timmy; and my meeting with Mary Martha. "So I've completed any immediate agenda I might have had," I continued. "The past doesn't draw me anymore. The future does and, after all, I have to *do* something, don't I? I was wondering if there was some way I might be of service, or at least begin to be trained to be of service."

"You feel ready to serve?" Sam echoed.

"He sure has moved fast, hasn't he?" Norma commented.

"I don't know whether it's fast or not, but yes, I do feel ready to serve. Like you. Maybe I could become a Greeter. I keep hearing about committees. Maybe there's some kind of committee work I might help with."

"It sounds like it's about time he met Isabel," Sam said. "What do you think, Norma?"

"Oh, definitely. It's her place to step in now."

I felt excited. "Who's Isabel?" I asked eagerly.

"She's the one in charge of determining when souls in this sector have completed the Adjustment and, if they have, of referring them on," Norma answered.

"If you think we're skilled, wait till you meet her," Sam added.

I tried to ignore the potentially threatening implications of her skill. "Referring souls on?" I queried. "On to where?"

"Oh, she'll discuss that with you," Norma said. Then, realizing I was not feeling the least reassured, she went on, "Don't worry. We'll talk with her and have her here in just a matter of minutes. You know how time works in this place."

I did indeed. At least I'd not have long to wait.

"Speaking of time," Sam said, "if Isabel thinks he's completed the Adjustment, it'll be the fastest one we've ever had, won't it, Norma?"

"Oh, no question about it, Sam," Norma replied. Then to me she said, "Have fun. Bye now."

I attempted to say, "Thank you," but they were both gone even before I could speak the words in my mind.

I was very glad this Isabel would supposedly be showing up shortly. If she was to determine whether I'd completed my Adjustment, it sounded like an examination. When I was a youth, I'd taken exams in my stride. As I aged, however, they became more and more nerve-racking. There were fewer of them, of course, but each time the stakes seemed to get higher. Today, for some reason I couldn't quite put my finger on, the stakes felt particularly high. I wanted her test to be over soon.

Norma had been correct. No more than ten minutes seemed to pass before a new light appeared in my little green room. Again, I was struck by how different these lights were. Although all the same size, each had its own subtle variations of color that radiated the soul's character. This soul was particularly intense. "You must be Isabel," I said, trying to project an image of affability that would not betray my anxiety. "Welcome."

"Thank you," she said. "Why are you so nervous?"

So much for my image! I explained to her about examinations.

"Ah, you're afraid I won't find you worthy," Isabel commented, "even though everyone in heaven is worthy. My examination is not about your worth; merely about timing. Is it the right time for you to complete your Adjustment? Sam and Norma told me you want to be of service."

"Yes."

"Why?"

The question surprised me. I'd thought that anyone in my position would want to be of service. I recounted what I'd done since arriving in my little green room and how it seemed time to me that I should start doing something useful.

"Doing, doing," Isabel noted. "So you want to be kept busy?"

"Not too busy." I gave her the history of the two parts of my nature that I hoped could stay in balance. "I do have a terror of boredom and like to work on projects that seem meaningful. I also have a terror of sleeplessness and need to have time when I do nothing except contemplate. I like vacations. Many people used to think I was a workaholic, but they never knew my hating to return from vacations."

The answer seemed to satisfy her. "You want there to be some meaningful work in heaven. That's understandable," she said. "But you'd told Sam and Norma you specifically wanted to be of service. Why service?"

"What other kind of work is meaningful?"

Isabel did not answer. I felt my question had been that of a smart aleck. With some embarrassment I began to elaborate. "I want to give to the world. Maybe it's love. I also want to pay back for what I've been given. I guess I want to try to pay back God."

"So that God will think you worthy?"

"Yes, that's part of it," I admitted with increasing embarrassment. "There's a certain sense in me that I need to earn God's love, even though I know that's poor theology. But it's deeper than that." Now I was really embarrassed. "You know, I had a fantasy that if I came to heaven I'd get to see God. It's been nice seeing you and Norma and Sam and Timmy and Mary Martha, but it hasn't felt like seeing God. I guess I hope that if I move on I'll see God."

"*See* God?"

"Yes, see God. Maybe that's a metaphor. Serve God. Be

close to God. Feel God. Love God. Worship God. Be loved by God. Touch God. Be friends with God. Know God. Speak with God. Participate in God. Be with God. They all seem to be wrapped up together. I don't know how to separate the pieces. I'm sorry."

Honest though it was, my answer seemed pathetically lame. I was therefore amazed when Isabel responded, "In three days' time—earth time, so to speak—you can move on if you still want to."

Indeed, I was so thunderstruck it did not occur to me to ask why the three days or what she meant by "if I still wanted to." All I could do was dumbly seek to clarify, "You mean my Adjustment will be over then?"

"Yes."

"You mean I can finally come home?"

"Yes, Daniel, you can finally come home."

I wept.

Isabel gave me time for my joy before proceeding. "I do need to ask you some more questions, however," she said. "Have you given thought to the way you'd most like to be of service?"

"In whatever way God most wants," I replied. "Or you. I gather you're God's representative in the matter."

"That's true. But tell me your fantasies."

"The only things I know enough to fantasize about are those I've actually experienced one way or another since I've been here," I said. "Norma and Sam have served me well, so naturally I've thought about possibly being a Greeter. With training I imagine I could probably do it well."

"Why do you imagine that?"

"Well, it strikes me it's very much like doing psychotherapy. I used to be a therapist back on earth before I got involved in other things. I wasn't the greatest of therapists, but I wasn't bad either."

"You got involved in other things?"

I knew what she was driving at. "Yes, writing and lecturing and social action work. And yes, I wouldn't have become so involved with them if I was completely satisfied as a psychotherapist. In fact, I was burnt-out well before I was fifty."

"I'm not sure God would want you in heaven to do something that you were long ago tired of on earth," Isabel commented mildly.

Suddenly I had a vision. Or was it a revelation? Granted to me by Isabel or God? God Himself or Herself? I'd been struck by how much Sam and Norma had seemed to be enjoying themselves. Could it be that they were, in fact, ordinary people doing what for them were extraordinary things? That for them their psychotherapeutic work was utterly new and exciting? I recalled them telling me very quickly that this realm was dominated by the Principle of Freedom. Could that mean that everyone in heaven was doing exactly and completely what he or she wanted to do? Although I now wanted to move on, ever since arriving here I'd been doing precisely what I wanted to do. And painful though it might be in her Pink Purgatory, wasn't Tish doing exactly what she wanted to do, needed to do? For that matter, however pathetic, the souls in hell were also doing just what they wanted to do.

On earth too I had done mostly as I'd wanted, but I'd also considered myself to be one of the very, very few lucky ones. By virtue of the body and its vicissitudes, greed and war, poverty and oppression, the prevailing view of existence was one of a generally futile gamble. This was such a different vision. Yet not unheard of. That strange lady, Dame Julian of Norwich, who had almost totally isolated herself in a specially built cell of a convent for decades, had written in the fourteenth century that, despite the inevitability, even the necessity, of sin, "All shall be well, all shall be well, and all manner of thing shall be well." I'd thrilled to her resounding proclamation, but at the same time I'd tossed it off with Marx as "pie in the sky, by and by." Now I was in the sky, or wherever, and it dawned on me that her "revelation of divine love" was the underlying reality.

"Yes, Julian was correct," Isabel noted, reading my mind.

But I was still mostly stuck in an earthly vision of a total universe wherein it was impossible for a "good" soul to do simply what she or he most wanted to do. "Perhaps I could work in hell," I offered. "God knows the people there could use some assistance. And back on earth I used to be considered something of an expert on such poor souls."

"Yes, you wrote well about them. But did you *like* working with them?"

"Lord, no!" I admitted. "They were the most difficult of all. Still, you could look at that as a challenge. Possibly I could discover some new techniques. It would take an enormous amount of patience. That's something I've never been very good at, however."

Since the stakes of this examination were obviously so high, it seemed essential for me to be totally honest with Isabel. I told her about my Daniel complex in all its ramifications. Given the fact that she could read my mind, the recounting did not take long. But at the end, because I was dealing with new material, I chose my words carefully.

"The last twenty or so years of my life on earth I realized that I was an unusually impatient person," I said, "but since coming here I've really had my nose rubbed in it. I've acted rudely—almost crazily—in my impatience to get at the answers, and the past few days have been the first time I've ever made the connection between my lack of patience and the whole Daniel business. I see now that it's rooted in anxiety. I'm so desperate to have the answers because I'm terrified that if I don't have them I'll make one of those missteps that'll plunge me into the lions' den. It's so silly. Perhaps working with the souls in hell would give me an opportunity to learn patience."

"A fine little piece of analysis," Isabel retorted, "but did it ever occur to you that maybe what God most needs from you is your impatience?"

I was completely taken aback. Isabel sounded for all the world like the beloved spiritual director I'd had on earth, a wise little nun who had a way of being consoling and confronting in the very same sentence. "You mean I don't have to be healed of my complex?" I sputtered.

"A complex, as you call it, is a neurosis only when it blocks your path. It's hardly something that needs healing when it speeds you on your way. So forget about plodding work in hell. Tell me what turns you on."

"Okay, let's take something I don't know anything about," I suggested. "Mary Martha serves on a committee that works on soul creation. She also said there are committees for soul nurturance. That's all new to me, and it seems terribly important. Critical. I was horrified at first when she described soul creation as experimentation, but the more I thought about it, the more exciting it sounded."

"Soul creation and nurturance are naturally in some ways

akin to mothering," Isabel informed me. "That doesn't mean men can't do it. There are many men who have fantasies of pregnancy and yearn for nothing else than child-care work. So there are men on those committees. Did you ever wish you could experience pregnancy?"

She had me pinned to the wall. "Never," I acknowledged. "Nor was I great at day-to-day child care the way Mary Martha was. I may not have been a bad father, but I could have been much better had I also been more of a mother. Patience again. I never had Mary Martha's extraordinary patience."

"Let's get something straight, Daniel," Isabel said emphatically. "You don't have the problem you think you have. You and Mary Martha were both patient and impatient, but each in your separate ways. It takes enormous patience to write a book, and you managed to write a dozen of them. Did she have that kind of patience?"

"Not until the end of her life when she felt called to write her memoirs."

"Exactly. We like to do what we are called to do, and we are very patient when we are doing what we like, when we are fulfilling a calling, when something fascinates us. Besides your books in general, for what were you most recognized back on earth?"

"Well, I was awarded a couple of peace prizes."

"And what about peacemaking fascinated you most?"

I did not have to search for the answer. "Culture," I replied. "I was raised in a crazy culture, and I was called to leave it. The same with Mary Martha. That meant we had to create our own culture, and one way or another for forty years I was involved in trying to help others create their own and better cultures: individuals, churches, business corporations, even governments and nations. I guess you could say that culture change was my passion."

"Then it seems obvious you might best serve God here on a culture change committee."

I was dumbfounded. "Culture change committee? You have culture change committees here?"

"Of course. We have something for everyone. Seriously, I'm surprised you haven't realized it. You know all the committees are involved, one way or another, in furthering the evolution of souls. That includes cultural evolution. Evolved souls create evolved cultures, just as you were trying to do on earth, and you worked so hard at it precisely because you knew that evolved cultures also help to create and nurture evolved souls. You know that with enormous care we delicately intervene in human affairs. Grace, you called it. You knew we not only intervene in the lives of individuals but also groups. Naturally—again very carefully—we occasionally make whole cultural interventions."

Isabel was correct. It was stupid of me not to have realized.

"Actually," she continued almost relentlessly, "there are many different committees to deal with different aspects of culture change. The most advanced, so to speak, focus their activities here in heaven. As you well know, culture change most properly begins at home. And at the top. Other committees focus purely on local cultures. Then there are those that focus primarily on cross-cultural operations of the kind that are most likely to foster intergroup or international peace. It seemed to me that your calling and experience might best suit you for one of those."

She'd had me pretty much figured out from the beginning, I thought. But no matter. I felt much more educated than manipulated, more grateful than chagrined. "Yes, I'd like that very much," I said.

"There are some things you ought to know before you jump at it," Isabel warned. "You'll need to learn a new language, for instance."

It did seem suddenly less attractive. "I've never been good at learning foreign languages," I said, crestfallen.

"Oh, poo. You just weren't motivated."

"Maybe," I countered, "but I also never seemed to have much of a knack for it the way some do."

"Motivation and calling again," Isabel snapped. "You used to proclaim that you had no knack for scholarship, but when you needed it to write one of your books, you'd delve into the most esoteric subjects with insatiable gusto. In fact, in one of your books you made a big point that you were no scholar when the whole book was filled with fine scholarship. You just didn't like to do footnotes."

My God, I wondered, did the woman know everything about me? Had she read everything I'd written?

"Yes, we do some research here in heaven," Isabel answered my thoughts. "When we're motivated. And I suspect you'll be motivated to learn this new language. Haven't you found it remarkable that everyone you've talked to here so far has been American?"

"It does seem remarkable now you've pointed it out. I was too dumb to think of it before," I replied. "Statistically, I should have expected Greeters who were Chinese or Hindu, but I guess that wouldn't have done, would it?"

"No, it wouldn't. As spirit you can hear minds now and, without study, you'll quickly become adept at reading them, but you'll still only be able to read them in English. If you're going to do cross-cultural or international work, you've obviously got to learn an international language that transcends culture."

"A universal language like Esperanto?"

"Yes and no. Mostly no. We encouraged Esperanto because it established the concept of an international language. Otherwise it failed, as we knew it would. For many reasons. It was way before its time. People didn't have the motivation to learn it. It wasn't really universal; it was European and had nothing to do with Asia or Africa. Finally, it wasn't cross-cultural. It had no way to translate idioms that would make sense across cultures."

I was beginning to get excited. "But here you have a universal human language that does succeed?" I asked eagerly, "And how does it? How does it work?"

"It succeeds perfectly," Isabel pronounced. "As to how and why it does, that's impossible to adequately describe until you actually get into learning, practicing, and using it. Part of it is learning myths because it uses a shared mythology. Primarily it works because it's nonverbal. It's more like music than words."

"I've never been good at music either," I moaned—or was it whined?

"Whether it's a neurotic complex or not, you really do have a habit of getting in your own way sometimes, don't you?" she noted tartly. "If I remember correctly, you took up the violin at the age of fifty only to drop it as soon as you realized you in fact could learn to play it rather well. And one of the reasons you were so successful on the lecture circuit was that you used to sing to your audiences. Often solo."

"But not well," I pointed out. "Oh, they said I had a good voice and sang well, but I really didn't."

"Oh, Lord, Daniel's got to be perfect, doesn't he? Every time, every moment, just like his obnoxious namesake."

"I'll try, Isabel," I said. "I'll try to learn this new language. That's all I can promise."

Perhaps she appreciated my habitual reluctance to make a commitment I wasn't certain I could fulfill, because she suddenly turned reassuring. "It's not entirely easy to learn," she acknowledged. "It's complicated. Yet in only a few days you'll get a taste for it, and then it will be almost addicting. It's aesthetic. Far better than English, and no earthly language is more rich than English. You can't imagine how elegant it is. If the two of us could use it now, it would be like bathing in delight. Besides, you'll need to learn it sooner or later. Everyone here eventually does."

Dumb though I was, I finally picked up on something. "Obviously you've learned it," I said, "or you wouldn't be able to talk about it with such enthusiasm."

"Yes, I've learned it."

"How old are you, Isabel? I hope you don't mind my asking. How long have you been here?"

"I was born in Rhode Island in 1683," she answered me. "I 'died' when I was nineteen. It was 1702. From diphtheria, although I was also married and pregnant at the time. So I've been here close to three hundred years now, as has my baby."

I was in awe.

Although she'd shown no reluctance to tell me this much about herself, Isabel demonstrated no eagerness to say more. "There are two other things that might make you pause at concluding your Adjustment," she continued. "If you accept the assignment to one of the international culture change committees, you'll be starting at the bottom, you know. You won't even be a full apprentice. You'll be what we call a junior apprentice. That might be hard to take for a man who was so successful back on earth."

Here she'd read me wrong. "The attainment of power was never my primary motive back on earth," I responded. "Insofar as I wanted it, it was always to fulfill some greater objective, and by the last twenty years of my life—after I'd become successful, as you put it—I couldn't have cared less about power. I'm uneasy about my capacity to learn this new language, but the overall notion of being a full-time student again is actually a turn-on for me. No, I suspect I'll be quite content in the role of a junior apprentice."

"Just checking," Isabel said. "And I don't want to scare you. There's nothing drastic about a wrong assignment. If you're unhappy as an apprentice on this committee, then you'll simply be able to move to another, and we'll all be the wiser for it. The Principle of Freedom, remember? Everyone here is free to do exactly what she or he most wants to do."

I might have guessed it, but the notion of such freedom was still alien to me. After all, I'd spent my entire life in a world that obsessed over making the wrong choice. The wrong choice of college. The wrong choice of a job. Of a mate. Of an answer on an exam. The wrong choice of a car, a mechanic, a physician, or a drug, as if the consequences would always be permanent and unredeemable. "It's incredibly reassuring, this Principle of Freedom," I noted.

"Yet there are a few limits to it," Isabel elaborated. "Like you've been told, we're not free to interfere with earthly affairs in any way one of us just feels like. We do occasionally intervene, yes, but it's always done by committee with great caution. And now you're facing another limit. You'll need to give up this room. When people complete their Adjustment, we expect them to give up their rooms. How do you feel about that?"

"Queasy. Not unwilling, but a bit queasy," I answered. Mary Martha had prepared me for it. Being with her in the void had been most pleasant. Being alone had been less so, but not intolerable. I could do it. "It only makes sense," I went on. "I know there are souls praying these rooms into existence. Such round-the-clock prayer must take a great deal of energy. It would be ridiculous to expend that kind of energy on something that isn't really needed. I did need it at first, but I'll be happy to give up the room to a new soul to begin his or her Adjustment. I can live in the void whenever necessary. As long as I can sleep when I'm tired, I don't need a specific place to do it in."

"Still, the thought of giving it up does make you a bit queasy," Isabel probed.

"I've got something of an addictive personality," I explained. "I get attached to my little comforts. I know it's silly to be attached to a tiny, barren room, but it's been something. Something that's mine. Without it I suspect I'm going to feel kind of homeless for a while."

"Even though, as we talked about, you'll be coming home?"

"I suspect so," I admitted.

"That's natural," Isabel reassured me. There was a hint of gaiety in her tone. "It's one of the natural paradoxes of existence: we're not ready to come to our true home until we're truly ready to be homeless."

She gave me only a moment to absorb the paradox before she abruptly proclaimed, "I'm going to leave you now. I'll be back to see you in three days. By then you'll know whether you're truly ready."

"Wait," I pleaded. I practically clutched at her, but, of course, one cannot cling to a soul. "What should I do between now and then? What do you suggest I do to prepare myself?"

"Pray and be careful," Isabel said . . . and was gone.

I kicked myself for not asking her the reason for the three-day wait. Why the delay? She could read my mind. Couldn't she tell that I was ready *now?* That there was nothing to keep me from moving on?

I considered trying to call her back. It occurred to me, however, that one does not argue with, much less summon, a soul that's been around for over three hundred years. And Isabel had clearly been around, so to speak. From the fact she had told me I was to be a junior apprentice, it was clear there was some sort of power hierarchy in heaven. Where she fell in that hierarchy, I didn't know, but it was obviously not at an apprentice level. So I settled down to do what she'd suggested: pray.

There are thousands of ways to pray, and I'd fancied myself as being rather good at them. Consequently, I was not bothered that I didn't have the foggiest idea what to pray for. The prayers of the unknowing are at least as sweet to God as any others. Gradually, my prayer became focused on Isabel's other instruction. "Be careful," she'd told me. Why? Was this a time when I should be particularly careful? Careful about what? I didn't know, but I knew to pray for carefulness.

Praying for carefulness, I began to wonder what it was I

might already be full of care about. God was the immediate answer. More than anything else, I cared about God, the very One I prayed to. Was there anything else I cared about? People. Mary Martha and Timmy. My children and grandchildren left on earth. Friends left on earth. New friends here. Sam and Norma and now Isabel. And those who were not exactly friends, like Tish. Even the souls in hell, each and every one of them. I cared for the whole of our struggling infant humanity. And it went further than that. Yes, I cared for the wolves and the whales, the rain forests and the earth, the entire panoply of God's creation. Caring for God was inseparable from caring for creation. And evolution. This wasn't something I just believed; it was something I knew. And to think that shortly, however small, I would have a role in evolution! In one sense, life just goes on.

Yet something was missing from my contemplation. Something like creation and evolution, both separable and inseparable from God. What? It was truth. By some act of grace, as far back as I could remember, I had worshiped the truth. I didn't always know what the truth was, but I cared so deeply about it that I instinctively hated a lie whenever I discerned it in others or in myself. I'd not lied to another since my childhood, but I knew I still had the capacity to lie to myself in subtle ways. Be careful. Full of care. "Oh, Lord," I prayed, "protect me from falsehood."

CHAPTER

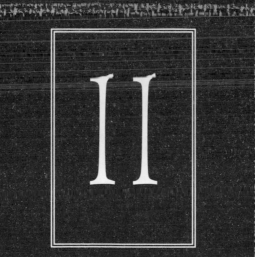

*S*ome prayer can be exhausting; some boring; and some both. I'd fallen asleep praying, and now I awoke praying. It occurred to me that my situation was analogous to that of monks and nuns who were required to make a lengthy, silent retreat in solitude prior to taking their monastic vows. It was a time of testing. And a time of preparation. It now seemed quite proper that Isabel had directed this brief waiting period. I prayed that I would be well prepared.

Suddenly my little green room was almost entirely filled with a great bright light. The lights of Timmy, of Sam and Norma, and even of Isabel had all been similar in size. Why was this so huge? It was a powerful personage, I could tell. It had an overwhelming presence. Perhaps because it was so overwhelming, I could not discern its sex or sense anything about its personality otherwise. The fact that I had expected this to be a time of solitude made the presence even more astonishing. "Who are you?" I asked.

"Susan."

"Why is your light so large?"

"Because I'm very powerful . . . and very old," Susan answered. "For instance, I lived in Britain at least a thousand years ago."

"What brings you here?"

"I've come to take you on a journey. It's a part of your preparation."

I was cautious. "A journey to where?"

"It's a surprise," Susan said. "Don't you like surprises? *I* do. But don't be afraid. It's to a place on earth that you love—a place that was very special to you."

"I dunno," I responded, shrinking back dubiously. I neither had the desire to return to earth nor any understanding as to why it should be a necessary part of my preparation.

"Of course you're reluctant," Susan acknowledged. "Didn't Isabel instruct you to be careful? And well she should have. One doesn't usually just run off with strangers. But I assure you that if the place I'm taking you to isn't right for you, you can instantly return here just by wishing it. The Principle of Freedom, you know. And there's no one—I repeat, no one—who understands more about the Principle of Freedom than I do. Or respects it more. So come along."

What could be the harm of it? It seemed one of those times when my Daniel complex was simply getting in my way. This powerful personage knew about Isabel and approved. She reminded me and assured me about the Principle of Freedom. I was feeling ridiculously stodgy and unadventurous. "All right," I agreed. "I'll go with you."

The next moment I was sitting in a copse of pine trees on the top of a hill gazing down over a medieval town built into the hillside and further out across a great plain that shimmered in the summer sunshine. The peace of the place was palpable. I could even hear the insects in the air. I knew exactly where I was, of course: Assisi. Directly below, at the edge of the town, was St. Francis's basilica. Soon there would be bells. Twice in my life before I had sat in this precise same spot. Susan had been correct: it had been a very special place for me indeed.

But where was Susan? I looked to the left, then to the right, and that was when I first became truly conscious of my chromosomes. Every single cell in my body went on alert. Five feet to my right there was a girl, a woman, in between, maybe eighteen. She was sitting as I was sitting, her knees drawn almost up to her chin, her hands clasped in front of them. I saw her in profile. Softly curled, her hair—hard to name whether it was blond or brown—was cropped short so as not to distract from, only to emphasize, the perfectly straight bridge of her nose and the roundedness of her lips. She looked so tangible I assumed she was a person of the earth; either an Italian girl from the town or else a tourist.

I wondered whether my sudden appearance might have violated her privacy. Without thinking that she could probably neither see nor hear me, I said, "Excuse me. It's a beautiful view, and I hope I'm not interrupting your enjoyment of it."

"Of course you aren't," she responded, turning to me with one of those smiles of both lips and eyes by which beautiful young women are so accustomed to light up the world. "You're hardly interfering with my enjoyment when I brought you here so we could enjoy it together."

"You're Susan?" I exclaimed. "But you look so real!"

"That's because I am real, silly."

I examined her more closely. She was wearing sandals and tight-fitting faded blue jeans. She had no belt. A white shirt tucked into her jeans had its button-down collar open to frame her delicate neck. The shirt was very clean, I noted for some reason. It was loose and merely suggested her breasts. She reminded me of a couple of girls I had dated in my teens when my groping sexuality was pathetically inexperienced. And of the teenage girls I would ogle in my thirties thinking, "If I only knew then what I know now." But it was more than that. Susan had the kind of grace that made her exactly the sort of woman who had come to me several times in my dreams only to leave me to awaken with hopeless yearning.

"You're so real," I repeated dumbly.

"And you are too," Susan proclaimed. "Look at yourself. Touch yourself."

I did so. I could see my feet! They were encased in a pair of topsiders. I wasn't wearing socks, so my ankles were visible between them and the bottom of my jeans. I looked for my hands and found them. And my forearms as well since I was in a polo shirt. They were tanned. To my amazement I realized that the skin was tight and smooth. No wrinkles or blotches. No horned, ribbed fingernails, bulging knuckles, or crooked veins. "My God," I said, "my hands look almost as young as yours."

"They are," Susan told me. "And the rest of you as well. Your body is just as it was the day you graduated from high school."

"My mind?"

"No, your mind is grown-up. You have all your knowledge and wisdom. It's like a fantasy, isn't it?"

"But why? How?" I stammered.

"Would you mind me being closer while I tell you?"

"Of course not."

She edged herself sideways along the ground of fallen pine needles until our buttocks were almost touching. I looked down at her left thigh, no more than three inches from mine, and pleasured in its gentle swelling before it tapered away to her knee. "I wanted your body to be the way it was at its best," she explained.

"So you've done this?" I queried. "You've brought my body back to life, so to speak?"

"Yes, and I can keep it this way forever."

"You have that power?"

Susan smiled at me almost shyly. "I'm very powerful, Daniel," she said. "I told you that."

"But why? Why me?"

"Because I love you, Daniel. I've loved you since the day you were born. I've watched you every day of your life, and wanted you every day. It seems I've wanted you for a thousand years, and now you're finally ready for me."

"I still don't understand," I said, pleased yet skeptical. "Why me? Me specifically?"

"Who's to explain love?" Susan countered. "We're soulmates, that's all. It's just the way it is. We were made for each other since the beginning of time."

I remained skeptical. From late adolescence on I had distrusted the notion of soulmates. Yet at this moment I was closer to believing in it than I ever had been. In my imagination I had concocted the most desirable women I possibly could, and they all resembled Susan one way or another.

Still, these mental creations of mine had been but fantasies, always slightly off the mark, and now, only now, it was as if I had finally hit the bull's-eye. Or the bull's-eye had hit me. How to explain that we might be real soulmates? "Tell me more about yourself," I asked. "You said that you were over a thousand years old? That you came from Britain?"

Susan made a wry face. "Oh, Daniel, I don't want to talk about the past. Not now. I told you I've wanted you for a thousand years. Not just for talk. I've wanted *you*. I want you *now*. We can talk about the past later. We've got a world of time together. Besides, you want to talk about the past so much because you really don't believe me yet, do you? You want the past to explain it for you, don't you, you ever so reasonable, scientific, rational man?"

I nodded. She'd discerned my motives.

"You're still thinking this is all unreal, aren't you?" she continued. "You're not sure I'm real. You're not even sure I've actually brought your body back to life. Would you like me to show you how alive you are?"

I nodded again. I was willing to go almost anywhere she wanted to lead me.

I wasn't prepared, however, for what happened next. She began to unbutton her shirt. She did it slowly, not out of reluctance but the most obvious deliberateness. She was wearing no brassiere. She did not stop in the midst to tantalize me. She went down to her waist and to the bottom button underneath her jeans. Then she methodically, inexorably turned to her cuffs. When they were undone, she quite calmly pulled out her arms, yanked the shirt free, and tossed it to her side. Her whole torso was naked for me.

I had three separable, ongoing reactions.

Perhaps the most dramatic, because it seemed to have absolutely nothing to do with my mind, was the stirring in my loins. A delicate term. The fact is that I could feel the blood deluging into them within five seconds of her starting. She had convinced me that my body was alive indeed.

But at what cost? A second reaction was astonishment at the blatant provocativeness of Susan's action. Never had a new woman I'd not paid for simply unbared herself for me for sexual reasons without the slightest foreplay. The term "shameless hussy" sprang into my mind as involuntarily as my erection sprang into the sadly limited space of my crotch. Was my supposed soulmate nothing but a whore?

So one purely physical and one purely intellectual reaction. The third, I suppose, was mixed. I was in awe. Susan's breasts were just on the small size of average—and just as I would desire on a soulmate. Her nipples stood out on their own as if filled with some sort of mystical fluid, their tips pointing upward. I had seen breasts like this before in wonder. How could they be so substantial and still reach upward toward my eyes, as if to defy every facet of gravity? I desperately wanted to cup them in my palms.

"Yes, you can touch them," Susan said. "Just for a moment. Go ahead and touch. Feel how real I am."

I cupped my left hand around the bottom and inner portion of her left breast which fit into my palm as if it had been created for that very purpose. Yes, it felt real, that reality more real than real, that flabbergasting paradox of a woman's breast whereby it is unutterably soft and firm at the same time. "Oh, God," I moaned as I began to drop my head to take her nipple in my mouth.

Susan pulled her torso away. "No kissing," she said. "Not

until we have an agreement. Then you can kiss all you want."

"An agreement?"

"Yes. I need you to worship me."

I began to be on guard. "Worship you?"

"Of course. That's what women want, isn't it? To be worshiped? You must have known that. It's different for men. They mostly want to be admired. A woman doesn't care so much about being admirable. What she wants is to be worshiped. She wants to belong to a man, and she'll do anything for him as long as she's his goddess."

I recognized there might be some truth in this. "I feel as if I am worshiping you," I responded, looking hungrily at her breasts. And her lips. And her fingertips. She wore no nail polish, no lipstick, no makeup whatsoever; she needed none. I desperately wanted to worship her with my mouth.

"Let him kiss me with the kisses of his mouth!" she intoned from the Song of Solomon, reading my mind and inflaming me all the more. "I know you feel you're worshiping me now, Daniel, but feelings are cheap. I need a commitment. Just say it. Just tell me you'll worship me forever, and then you can kiss me. You can kiss me all over. Wherever you like. I want you to kiss me everywhere, but promise me first."

"I can worship at you," I told her truthfully.

"No, that's not the same. I don't want you to worship at me. I want you to worship *me*."

It was so strange. Here we were having an argument and my erection was still bulging against my pants unperturbed. During the last twenty years of my life I couldn't even maintain an erection in the midst of love, and here it was being maintained for me in the midst of strife. Or being maintained against me. My body truly was eighteen again, with testosterone crashing through my veins as much like a foe as a friend. "I can't worship you," I said. "I can only worship God."

"Oh, Daniel, dear Daniel," Susan crooned. "Don't you realize that I'm as close to God as you'll ever get? I'll bet that Isabel told you you'll be with God. On a committee? Did you really believe her? Did you honestly believe you'll be close to God on a committee?"

It did sound stupid. But no more stupid than Susan herself. "You not only want me to worship you," I pointed out, "but you wanted me to promise to worship you forever. I can't promise anything forever. Do you think I want to stay on this hilltop forever? That I'll want to make love to you every minute for eternity? That I'd be happy spending my entire life in some sort of unending Garden of Eden? Even with you? I need a life, Susan. I need to get on with it. Let's make love now. Then let me go, and we'll come back together whenever we can."

"No, Daniel, that's not the way it works."

At this point Susan suddenly shifted herself so that she was sitting in a lotus position facing me. For the first time I observed that she had large hips—the kind of hips that can drive me wild. But then she did something to drive me wilder. She placed her left hand on my lap and, first with her palm and then with her long clean fingers, she began to stroke me through the denim of my jeans. "You make it sound ugly," she said softly. "You make it sound as if a lifetime together on this hilltop—or wherever we went—would be an illusion. You talk about wanting to get on with it. That's the illusion. There is no *it* to get on with. The future is the illusion. I'll bet that Isabel also told you you'd be learning this beautiful new language. It's not beautiful; it's tedious. She tried to downplay that, didn't she? A beautiful language, hah! What could be more beautiful than the language of love?"

"I dunno," I said miserably.

Susan took her right hand and began to unzip my fly. "I'm going to show you something that's not an illusion," she said.

I jerked away no more than an ineffectual inch. "Someone might see us," I protested.

"Nobody can see us. We're invisible to earthlings. I promise."

I let her go ahead to do what she wanted to do. She had to tug this way and stretch that but, finally, like a newborn, she delivered its body into the air. I thrilled to it almost as much as to Susan's breasts. As an adolescent I'd thought of myself erect as a shameful thing, perhaps to be willingly fondled by a woman in the dark yet nothing to be gazed at in rapture. But I had learned differently, and now my own narcissism echoed Susan as she exclaimed over it, "It's beautiful, Daniel. I knew it would be like this."

I began to roll over to reach for her, but she held me back. "Just say it, Daniel," she pleaded. "Just say you'll worship me forever. Don't you think that I want our tongues to taste each other? Don't you think I want to be licked and sucked? That I want to be taken and entered? Please, Daniel, just say it."

I was aware of three things. I was aware that I desperately wanted to just say it. I was aware that it would be a lie. And I was aware that I couldn't think.

Reluctantly, I took Susan's sweet hands from my lap and

placed them on her own. "I can't think," I told her. "I have to get away. I want to go to my little green room. You said I could go back. That I had the freedom. Maybe it will be just for a few minutes. I have to get out of this body and be alone for just a few minutes so I can think. Then I'll come back and give you my answer. I promise you I'll come back."

"No," she said firmly, suddenly radiating her power. "Yes, you can forsake this body I've returned to you. Yes, you can also flee to your little green room. But the Principle of Freedom applies to me also. If you leave now, I won't be here when you come back. That's *my* promise. You'll never see me again."

I believed her. I couldn't leave because I couldn't bear the thought of never making love to her. But I had to think. So I did the only thing that I could. I leaped to my feet and stumbled to the nearest pine tree. I encircled it with my arms lest she try to pull me away and buried my face against it so I couldn't see her. I also pushed my bared erection against the sharp bark in the hope the pain would make it go away. It didn't work. But at least I was able to pray, half sobbing. "Dear Lord God, Lord Jesus, help me to think."

At first nothing seemed to happen. But then I was aware of a fourth thing. I was aware of how the day before I had prayed for protection from falsehood. I prayed for it again: "Dear Lord, protect me from falsehood."

The next thing that happened was that I became aware this protection thus far had worked. Thus far I had been unwilling to lie to Susan. I had not yet spoken falsehood. I had not told her I would worship her, much less forever. The realization felt strengthening.

Next it occurred to me that I might need protection not

only from my own falsehood but also the falsehood of others. What others? From Susan? Had she been lying to me?

At that point, I actually became able to think once again. No, I couldn't quite say that Susan had lied to me, but I also couldn't say she'd told me anything that was true either. She had, in fact, been remarkably evasive. She'd said nothing about how she'd given me back my body. It was clearly my old body, yet she'd also told me that it was invisible. How could that be? Or was this body that was so much my body with its young familiar hands and same genitals and all its testosterone nothing but an incredibly powerful illusion? I didn't know. I was starting to think again but didn't yet know what to think.

As to why she'd singled me out, Susan had simply declared us soulmates, as if that explained everything. Maybe it could if the notion was in any way scientifically or even theologically substantiated, but it wasn't. It was a most doubtful notion and hence a most dubious explanation. Not demonstrably false, but certainly not demonstrably true.

My thoughts were interrupted by Susan's voice cooing behind me. "Come back, Danny. Come here next to me again. There's no need for you to go through all this agony. It's not a big deal."

Perhaps it was her use of "Danny"—as Mary Martha might have called me—that gave me the small spark of anger I needed to respond. "Shut up! It is a big deal." I took my arms from around the tree to put my fingers in my ears, forcing myself to think.

Falsehood! Was there more falsehood? Yes, there was her attitude toward Isabel. At the beginning, when Susan had first appeared in my little green room, she seemed to approve of Isabel. But here, when I wouldn't promise eternal worship, Susan had denounced her as a liar for telling me that I'd be closer to God doing committee work and that the new language I'd learn would be beautiful. Who was the liar? Isabel? Or was it Susan—Susan who had proclaimed the future to be an illusion? If the future was an illusion, why had God bothered to keep my soul alive? Even provide me with my little green room?

These speculations, however, seemed almost minor as I focused on Susan's background. What had she told me about her history other than that she had lived in Britain at least a thousand years ago? I'd taken that to mean she'd been born there in the ninth century or so. But it didn't necessarily mean that at all. And when I'd requested her to provide me with more history, she'd put me off, moved closer, and started to undress. One could conclude that she was being subtle or I was remarkably stupid. Probably I'd been stupid. The truth was I didn't have the foggiest idea when she'd been born or where she'd come from.

And that was the moment when I guessed the reality.

I dropped my arms and turned back to face her. With my guess I had finally begun to detumesce. Looking at her again, however—she was standing now, her breasts still proud, but her posture hinting of hurt, like that of a forlorn waif—I began to swell once more. Still, I hardly noticed. I am as relentless as a bloodhound when I am on the trail of deception. "You said you were living in Britain at least a thousand years ago."

"Yes," she answered, eyes all downcast and demure.

"How about two thousand years ago?" I interrogated. "Did you also exist in Britain two thousand years ago?"

Now her eyes began to flash as she looked at me directly. "Yes."

I bored ahead. "And what about three thousand years ago? Were you around in Egypt three thousand years ago?"

"Yes."

"Are you a human being or are you an angel?" I demanded. "I want the truth now. I won't believe your lies. The truth."

"I'm an angel."

"You're not Susan," I proclaimed. "That's been a lie too, hasn't it? Sounds alike: Susan/Satan. You're Satan. Admit it. You're Satan, aren't you?"

Instead of answering me, she turned and bent down to unbuckle her sandals . . . or was it to show me her full buttocks bursting at the tight denim of her jeans? I was throbbing. Averting my eyes, I tried to squeeze my erection back inside my fly without success. I was starting to unbutton my pants to get it back when she turned back to me and ever so slowly began to unbutton *her* jeans. I could no longer not look. I was mesmerized by the revealed white triangle of her panties. With the same slow deliberateness, she hooked her thumbs into the waistline of her jeans and, shimmering slightly, guided them down to her knees and let them fall to her feet. Stepping out of them, she moved forward half the distance between us.

I gawked. She had that wonderfully wide kind of pelvis where her thighs did not quite touch each other at their tops, leaving a slight opening below her panties that I could actually see through. Above it, her panties bulged faintly toward me from the pressure of her mons. "You want me to take them off, don't you?" she said, gazing at me with eyes of seeming innocence. "You want to see what's behind them."

I did not answer.

I could hardly breathe. As if in loving kindness, she slowly slid the panties down her thighs, let them drop to her feet, straightened up, and stepped out of them and forward even closer to me, her arms outstretched. I was transfixed by the sight of her pubic hair, thick and brown and deep, beckoning to me. "Just say it, Danny," she said. "Just say it. That's all you have to do."

I was not going to. I had only two decent choices. One was to wish myself back to my little green room in the terror of escape, but I knew if I did so I would be forever haunted by this beckoning image, this vision of her. My only other option was to destroy the image. I prayed for authority. "In the name of God and of Jesus Christ and all that's true and holy," I shouted, "I order you to reveal yourself for who you are."

She gave me a slight smirk. "You want me to reveal myself, Danny? All right." She dropped her outstretched arms and, thrusting her hips forward, with her fingers pulled apart her labia as if to spread herself open for me, welcoming and inviting.

I remained as enchanted and desirous as ever. But for the very first time I now also became fully angry. It was a cold anger. I dropped my voice. "You know that is not what I meant," I said evenly. "You will not reveal your body anymore. You will reveal your true self. You will drop all your disguises. You are Satan. You will appear to me as you are, and you will do it now. This I command you and this God commands you."

The revelation was not gradual; it was instantaneous. The slight smirk on her face was no longer slight. It turned into a wide grin, not of joy but of maliciousness, a grimace of overweening pride, a sneer of vicious superciliousness. It was a face of pure, subhuman hatred, and the only true gift she had given me. Vaguely aware that her body had vanished leaving only the grimace like the Cheshire cat in Wonderland, I peered at it, praying that it would be this visage I most remembered. I did so because I knew that she hated me. It was not that she hated me now I had rejected her. The reality was that she had hated me from the beginning. I knew not why, but I did know that she had come to me in hatred, and I wanted to remember that.

"Dear Lord," I prayed, "please get me out of this body and back to my room."

It reminded me of my first arrival. The unrelieved green of the little room seemed as foreign as if I'd suddenly awoken in a stateroom of an alien spaceship. One might think I'd be accustomed to not having a body now, but it felt strange to have no hands or feet. It wasn't frightening, as it had been in the beginning. Nevertheless if I didn't miss most of it I had to admit a certain sense of loss that my young manhood was gone after its brief reappearance. I did not, however, miss the testosterone. How strange that God—or evolution—should give us a thinking brain as well as hormones to short-circuit it!

So my predominant reaction was relief that I could think. And a sense I had been spared. What would have happened had I said yes to Susan, that I would worship her forever? I doubted that I would still be thinking in any decent sense of the word.

Of course, it wasn't really Susan at all. Now that I could think again, I recalled my lack of any sense of sexuality emanating from the great light that had entered this room un-bidden. I'd not been deceived by a woman but by an It pre-tending to be a woman—an It who had the extraordinary power to seemingly bring my fantasies to life. It was not true femininity that had almost succeeded in seducing me so much as my own sexual fantasies.

But how clever of it! Damnably clever. Literally. I could have been damned for eternity. And I wasn't sure there was any other way it could have gotten to me. Once perhaps I could have been seduced by fame or power or money, but by luck or grace I'd outgrown their attractions. But I realized now I'd not outgrown sexual desire. That had died. Not been outgrown. My glands had shriveled, yes, but pump a little testosterone back in me and my judgment was reduced to that of an adolescent.

Could I blame it all on testosterone? Yes and no. Yes, it was a powerful chemical. But why its peculiar power in me when I knew so full well after year upon year of experience how it could lead me down the proverbial garden path? Why was sex my weak spot? My weakest spot?

I remembered Susan/Satan telling me, "Don't you realize that I'm as close to God as you'll ever get? I'll bet that Isabel told you you'll be with God. On a committee. Did you hon-estly believe you'd be close to God on a committee?"

In the company of the illusion of Susan—or the reality of a beautiful woman—I believed myself no closer to God than in the company of any person. Yet there was something about sex that made it feel like being with God for me. It was a palpable substitute for the presence of God, a God who had never been as palpable or present to me as I'd desired. I'd been close to selling out for a substitute, an idol. In a sense, it was my own yearning for God that was my weak spot.

And was it an accident that Satan had taken me to Assisi, a holy place, to tempt me? I doubted it.

I was exhausted after the encounter. "Dear Lord, darling Lord," I prayed, falling asleep, "thank You for protecting me from falsehood and illusion. I don't know whether by working on this committee I will feel any closer to You than I do now or ever have in my life. As long as I am reasonably certain I am doing Your work, that will be sufficient. Teach me that it is more important for You to feel close to me than I to revel in feeling close to You."

CHAPTER

12

I awoke with a sense of sadness. It was a familiar feeling that I'd experienced almost daily during the last fifteen years of my life on earth. It was the sadness of loss, of life slipping away. The loss of people, of old friends, and, above all, the loss of my best friend, Mary Martha, when she died. Even more it had been the loss of interests, of enthusiasm for the affairs of the world, for life itself, that by the end had mostly come to seem like an empty illusion or bag of toys I'd long outgrown.

It did not take me long to figure out why today I should have this sadness so dramatically for the first time since arriving in my little green room. It was Susan. An illusion that did not exist. I would always remember the hideous face of Satan revealed—who could forget?—and the hatred stamped upon it. I would always know that the illusion of Susan had been deliberately cooked up to harm me. Without my body or a molecule of testosterone within me I would never yearn for Susan again. Yet such is the perversity of my soul I was now experiencing a twinge of regret. Although I did not want it back in the least, I was still mourning its death, the demise of one more illusion.

But it was only a twinge, and as soon as I acknowledged it I was looking forward again, not backward. What was in store for me? Presumably Isabel would be coming for me tomorrow to take me to some unknown place where, as a junior apprentice, I would begin attempting to learn a new language. And if I succeeded I'd eventually be doing some kind of work for a committee that somehow tried to benefit international relations back on earth. It was all too abstract for me to fantasize about with any gusto.

Isabel's return was not abstract, however. I'd met her, experienced her potent spirit. She'd promised me to return on the morrow, and I knew her to be a person of her word. Would she conclude I'd passed the test? Speaking of test, I'd need to tell Isabel about Susan/Satan even though I was embarrassed at how close I'd come to failing. But why the test of Susan? I'd assumed that this empty period of yesterday and today was meant to be a time of preparation. I further assumed that Satan's visit constituted a necessary part of my preparation. But I was at a loss to know why it was necessary. I very much looked forward to asking Isabel.

Meanwhile, I had this one day left for my preparation. How to use it? Conceivably I might receive another visitation, but that was not a matter within my control. What was in my control? Isabel's advice to pray and be careful had stood me in good stead yesterday. Today I would continue to be careful. As for prayer, I felt pretty much prayed out. It occurred to me I was preparing for a departure, and I wondered if I had any metaphorical bags to pack. Much as I might miss my little green room, it had no stove to be checked, no windows to be closed, no water to be turned off, no tangible way to say goodbye to it. What about people? Were there people I needed to say goodbye to?

There were hundreds, thousands, I hadn't yet said hello to. My parents were the most obvious. I'd wondered how they were doing and prayed it was well, but I had no desire to actually see them. There were mountains for which I could apologize to them: the myriad of ways in which I'd taken them for granted and failed to empathize with them out of the arrogance of youth. There was possibly as much for which they could apologize to me: the endless emotional rejection I'd received for not fitting the rigid and remarkably narrow mold they had preestablished. Nevertheless well before I died on earth, I'd become reconciled to them in my heart, and I had every reason to assume in this gentle place that after death they'd become reconciled to me.

Gentle place? A place where Satan was hanging around, waiting to corrupt me and presumably others? A place where millions worked night and day inside garbage cans? Did I have reason to think it any more gentle than on earth save that here we were spared the body with its fleeting joys and not so fleeting pains or ravages? Well, there was instant space and time travel, all for free. And certainly, with the exception of Satan's assault, I'd been treated with extraordinary gentleness and consideration. A room had been prepared for me. I'd been greeted. My adjustment had been professionally facilitated. I'd been left free to roam at will. Timmy had come the instant I needed someone just like him. Mary

Martha had been glad to see me. Isabel had been sent to help me with "career planning." Yes, for me it had been a gentle place indeed.

But I was leaving it. At least this part of it with my little green room. And then it occurred to me that there was a goodbye I could make . . . that I needed to make . . . that I wanted to make. It was Tish. Timmy had reassured me she'd do well in her pink purgatory. But had she? Had this been a gentle place for her? I was frankly curious. And it was proper for me to say goodbye to the one person I'd met who had been sharing this place and time of adjustment with me.

I wished myself to the corridor outside her room. I suppose I could have wished myself directly into her room, but I didn't want to barge in on her. I made a knocking sound as before, expecting to be invited inside by her previous "Entrez." Instead, it was "Come in." I did so and found something else different. Tish was as huge as before, but all the rolls of fat were hidden by a loose flowing muumuu of a tasteful brown that went surprisingly well with the pink of her room.

"Who are you?" she asked.

I realized I'd made no effort to project my bodily image. "I'm sorry," I said, making the correction. "I'm Daniel."

"Oh, you're the man who came here just about the same time I did," she exclaimed with recognition.

"It's true. How are you doing, Tish?"

"All right, I guess."

"Just all right?"

"I still don't understand why they can't put TVs in these rooms. They like to think of this place as a hospital of some sort. Even in decent hospitals they have TV," she whined.

Was it my imagination that the whine didn't have quite as

much gusto in it as it had a week ago? "You said they think of this as a hospital?" I asked.

"Yes. A psychiatric hospital. A nut house. You're starting to fade, you know."

I apologized for my inconsideration. "It's easier for me to let my physical projection drop," I explained. "It takes concentration for me to keep it up, and I'm not very good at it. I'll work at it if you like, but if it doesn't bother you, I can pay better attention to you without it."

"Go ahead," she said. "Be yourself. I'm getting used to all you different light balls. They tell me I may even become one of you myself." She didn't sound enthusiastic over the project.

"They?" I inquired.

"Yes. The doctors and nurses. Oh, they don't call themselves that, and they'd never actually call this a hospital, but they all act like it is."

"And are they helping you?"

"I dunno. I guess they're not hurting me. Except for the lack of TV. Maybe that's a kind of subtle torture they use."

"So nothing's changed?"

"Not really."

I'd been a psychiatrist so long back on earth, it was difficult for me to not act like one. I had no wish to be identified with the "them"—whom Tish seemed to envision more as enemies than friends—or to take over their job. But it felt downright inhuman for me not to make note of the obvious. "One thing's changed," I said. "You're wearing a different dress from the time I saw you last. It looks nice."

Tish looked pleased. "Thank you."

"Why'd you make the change?"

"I guess it had something to do with group therapy," she reluctantly acknowledged.

"Group therapy?"

"Again, they don't call it that. 'Body image discussion' is their term for it. But it's plain old group therapy. Specialty therapy. We're a 'cripples' group.' "

"I'm not sure I understand."

"Their theory is that people who are crippled develop an extrastrong attachment to their body. Our lives center around our physical disfigurement. You'd think I'd be happy to be rid of my fat body, but they say I hold on to it because I was fat. It's like my whole identity was being fat. Like if I let go of my body I'd totally lose my identity."

Now I could no longer restrain the psychiatrist in me. I was too fascinated. "Nice theory," I commented, "but is it true?"

"I'm not sure it's true for me," Tish hedged, "but I've got to admit it's true for the others."

"Tell me."

"Well, there's another woman in the group who has multiple sclerosis. I mean, she had it. She died from it. Now she comes to group in her wheelchair. We tease her about it. She admits she died but she can't admit there's anything silly about bringing a wheelchair with her into the afterlife. But we don't tease her much; it's too powerful. It's like it's real. Not only for her but for the rest of us. I mean we look at her and we not only see her skinny, paralyzed legs, but we see her wheelchair too. And you'd see it yourself if you were there just as clearly as you can see my muumuu."

"Is that why you traded your tight dress for the loose muumuu?" I asked.

Tish seemed to be warming up to the subject despite herself. "Sort of. I didn't want the group to tease me the way they do Cecelia—she's the one in the wheelchair. I realized they'd be pointing out to me that my old dress only emphasized my obesity. So after the second session I changed into this one. I didn't want them on my back and thought I'd beat 'em to the punch. Smart, aren't I? But I think it was George even more than Cecelia who pushed me into it."

It had begun to dawn on me that Tish *was* smart—much smarter than she looked or usually acted. "Who's George?" I asked.

"Another one of us 'patients.' "

"And how is he crippled?"

"He isn't really," Tish replied. "That's the point. George is a black man."

"So?"

"So he's very angry about it. That's why he's stuck." Tish was really warming up now. "He thinks that being black is a disfigurement. Oh, he won't admit that. He keeps saying that black is beautiful and he's only angry at whites for treating him as if he were disfigured like a cripple. If he gives up his body, people won't see him as black anymore, and he feels as if he'd lose his identity. Again, that's not what he says. What he *says* is that it would be a betrayal of his people, his race. But what we keep telling him is that it seems to be more important for him to be black than to be human."

"I can see how that's a bind for him," I commented with my psychiatrist's studied neutrality. Meanwhile, what I was thinking was how brilliant it was, almost as if they had deliberately created the perfect type of therapy for Tish. "How did you start going to the group?" I inquired.

"*They* suggested it. At first I didn't want to have anything to do with it. But they refused to suggest anything else, and finally I gave in just because I was so bored here with nothing else to do. It's entertainment. But I'm still not sure I'd go if Billy didn't take me."

"Billy?"

"Yes, he's a 'light ball' like you've become. I suppose he's my therapist, although he prefers to call himself my companion. Anyway, he comes here every morning to take me to group and brings me back when it's over."

"Like an aide or escort?"

"Well, he's a bit more than that. There are nine of us in the group at the moment. Each one of us has our own light ball. They sit with us while the group goes on. Behind each one of us actually. They practically never talk. They tell us that they're praying. Very occasionally they'll say something when we can't put a voice to our own feelings. Like George's light ball, for instance; she talks quite a bit. George is incredibly eloquent when he's talking about other people or his feelings about other people, but he gets absolutely tonguetied when it comes to talking of his feelings about himself. That's when she takes over. Generally he seems to appreciate it, but now and then he'll yell at her that he doesn't want to hear it and tells her to shut up."

"And does she? Does she shut up?"

"Of course."

"Who leads the group?" I asked.

Tish looked nonplused. "You know, I haven't thought about that. No one seems to. No one's designated the leader. I suppose we cripples or patients lead it ourselves. Maybe our light balls do. I guess you could say that we all somehow lead it together."

I was struck by the seeming cost-ineffectiveness of it. Nine therapists for nine patients in the same group! If this was therapy—and it seemed the very best—it was certainly more labor intensive than anything anybody had ever dreamed up on earth. Instinctively, I was thinking about how to economize. "Why don't you go to the sessions yourself?" I queried. "Do you really need Billy to get you there and back?"

"I guess not," Tish answered. "Billy's said I can go on my own when I feel ready, but he's not going to push it. I suppose someday I'll go by myself, but not yet. I know it sounds silly, but for some reason I'd be scared by myself."

I changed tack slightly to something that intrigued me. "You see this as some kind of psychiatric treatment," I remarked, "and I can understand why. Yet they seem to go to great pains to not label it as such, and that I don't understand."

"They try to explain it," Tish responded. "They think that psychiatry or words like treatment imply sickness, and they keep insisting that we're not sick. They believe that anyone who had our kind of bodies on earth would have our kind of difficulties adjusting to not having them here. They also point out that if you're sick, you ought to get well as quickly as possible. That's why psychotherapists back on earth are always pushing for rapid progress or improvement. Here they love to tell us that we've got all the time in the world and couldn't care less how fast we adjust. 'Your own pace' is their favorite catch phrase. That and the Principle of Freedom."

It was incredibly clever, I thought. My own greatest failing as a therapist had been my impatience, seldom accepting my patients just as they were, always nudging them and expecting more of them. I wondered: had I really wanted them so urgently to get better for their sake, or was it for my own—to bolster my self-esteem through my "success rate"? And was it any wonder that so many of them seemed covertly rebellious or what I'd labeled as resistant! Tish was certainly a resistant sort of person yet she seemed to me to have already made as much progress in a week as many of my patients had made over the course of a year. How clever it was to offer the most labor intensive treatment imaginable and at the same time make no demands or expectations!

Or was clever the right word? It implied a potential for manipulation. There was a sort of manipulative school of treatment back on earth called paradoxical therapy. Truly there was something paradoxical about this profligacy with therapeutic attention without any corresponding expectations of improvement. But was it incredibly clever or incredibly loving? Earlier, I'd briefly questioned whether this was a gentle place. Taking patients to and from therapy and sitting with them one to one during it, praying for them yet requiring nothing of them struck me as gentleness beyond measure. I felt like crying.

Still, I had no illusions about Tish. "What else have you been doing?" I asked.

"What else is there? I told you this place is boring."

"Why don't you take a vacation then? Go back and visit earth."

"Do you think I want everybody to see how fat I am?"

"They won't be able to see you at all, Tish," I suggested. "I went back and they walked right through me. It took me by surprise, but it also made me all the more certain that I'm bodiless now."

"That's what Billy tells me too. He's offered to go back with me. Maybe I'll take him up on it someday. Go someplace where I could watch TV. And if I was convinced they really couldn't see me, we might even take in a show at Vegas. That was always a dream of mine."

The idea of Tish in a disembodied state of floating about in Las Vegas amused me. It was hardly my cup of tea, but I recognized that a week ago she wouldn't have even faintly considered such an adventure. "Sounds like a good idea," I commented.

"I'm glad you came back," Tish suddenly announced. "I've been feeling guilty about you and wanted to apologize."

"For what?"

"For asking you to make love to me when you were here before. I mean, you were a stranger. It was very undignified of me."

"I understood where you were coming from," I responded. Indeed, I did. Just yesterday I would have made love to a total stranger had she—it—not insisted that I worship her first. I had no doubt that Tish's need to be desired was at least as potent a force as testosterone.

Perhaps also because of yesterday I began to wonder more deeply whether it was possible for souls to make love without bodies. Might I somehow be able to penetrate the soul of Tish and metaphorically ejaculate something of myself into her? I had come to say goodbye to her. I would have liked to offer her a parting gift of love, a wordless gift that she could feel inside of her and experience as healing. But one way or another it didn't seem workable. There was nothing erotic about it. Absent of my body and its hormones, there was no desire. Had Tish looked as Susan there still would have been none. I'd begun to like Tish—her soul—now she was distinctly growing in character, but I had no feeling of *need* to meld with her soul or anyone's. And was that not what making love was about? A melding, a merging, a temporary and total evaporation of boundaries? As a psychiatrist I knew that people like Tish usually needed to strengthen their boundaries before it would be healthy to loosen them. And as a male I knew lovemaking increased the desire of most women to bond. It would hardly be fair to whet Tish's appetite for bonding when I was leaving the next day. Whether it was possible for pure souls here to make love in any sense that I could conceptualize, I did not know. I doubted it. But I did know I wasn't going to attempt it with Tish.

"The reason I came to see you today," I announced, "is that I'm leaving here tomorrow." I told her very briefly that I'd be learning some kind of international language that would prepare me to serve on a committee. She didn't seem interested.

But as soon as I'd finished she astonished me by blurting out, "Give me a blessing."

"What?"

"I don't want you to leave before you give me your blessing."

"Why would you want my blessing?"

"I don't quite know," Tish answered. "I've never asked anyone else for a blessing. It just came to me to ask. I think it may be because you seem to me like a priest."

"I'm not a priest," I said quickly. "Years ago I used to be a psychiatrist. Then I became a writer."

"I don't care," Tish retorted. "There's something special about you, and I want your blessing."

I was embarrassed. It was not that I totally disbelieved in blessings. A colleague of mine once wrote that when psychotherapy succeeded it was often because the patient received a blessing of sorts from the therapist, a blessing the patient had failed to receive from his or her parents. That was certainly true of the psychoanalysis from which I had benefited, and it also held true for a number of my own cases. But such psychotherapy was lengthy and arduous. The therapist comes to know the patient in great depth. It is not a cheap blessing. Tish, however, I barely knew. We hadn't worked long and hard together. What she wanted was a quickie blessing, such as priests might give, and, as I'd pointed out to her, I was no priest.

"Well, are you going to give me one or aren't you?" she demanded, interrupting my musing.

"Hush," I commanded. "I'm trying to think."

One reason for my embarrassment was that this wasn't the first time I'd found myself in such a predicament. Twice before on earth relative strangers had come up to me asking for a blessing. They apparently believed there was something of the holy in me and that I had the power to create a miracle simply by laying my hands upon them. It was not a power I believed I possessed. Intellectually I supposed that God might work through me on occasion, but certainly not in ways over which I had any control. Because I hadn't wanted to reject them, I had touched those two supplicants and mumbled a few words, but I'd felt like a sham and, as far as I knew, no benefit had come to them. I was not willing to play the charlatan again. Besides, Tish had no real flesh for me to touch, and I had no hands to lay upon her.

"Do you believe in God?" I asked.

"I don't know," Tish replied. "I guess so. I've never thought much about it."

I stifled the urge to tease her for the incongruity of wanting my blessing while at the same time being an agnostic who'd never bothered to give God the time of day. Instead I responded, "Well, I do believe, and I think that all significant gifts come from God. If you're willing, I'll sit with you here and pray for about five minutes. Petitionary prayer. I'll petition God to give you a blessing. Okay?"

"I suppose so, if that's the best you can do."

I remembered a man back on earth years before who'd asked me to pray for something or the other. "You've got a direct line to God, Daniel," he'd said. That may have been his faith, but it wasn't mine. Nor my experience. My experience had taught me that only occasionally some prayer seemed to work. Certainly I had no direct line. "Prayer is funny stuff," I warned Tish. "On the one hand, I can't guarantee it will work. On the other, don't be disappointed if it seems not to. Sometimes good things can happen way later after the fact. God's schedule isn't necessarily ours, you know."

"Oh, stop lecturing and get on with it," Tish ordered.

I set aside my resentment at her haughtiness, knowing that behind it was mostly fear. Besides, her asking for a blessing was probably an act of humility. So I did get on with it and prayed in every way I knew how: with words and without; alternating fierce concentration with mental drifting; out of fullness and emptiness; pleading and exhorting. I was slightly more than halfway through this pious exercise when it was suddenly interrupted by Tish loudly exclaiming, "Well, I'll be damned!"

"What's the matter?"

"I don't know. It's the first time anything like that has happened to me."

It was also the first time I'd seen Tish obviously flustered. "Anything like what?" I asked, curious.

She turned on me angrily, trying to recover. "How did you do it to me?" she demanded.

"Do what?"

"Put that voice in my head."

"Tish, I don't know what you're talking about."

"You must have done it," she accused.

"Done what, damn it?"

My annoyance seemed to make her more reasonable. "I was just sitting here while you were praying—or whatever it was you were doing," she explained. "Just sitting, bored. Suddenly there was a voice inside my head. It didn't sound like you. I can't describe it. How do you describe voices? But it didn't seem to come from you the way it does when I hear you talking. Certainly it wasn't me. You must have done it somehow."

"What did the voice say?"

Tish turned red. "Not much." She was obviously embarrassed.

I tried swearing again. "Damn it, tell me what it said."

"It was just a sentence. I can't even tell you whether the voice was male or female. All it said was, 'You give me pleasure.' It was clear as a bell."

" 'You give me pleasure'?" I repeated dumbly.

"Yes. That's what it said. How did you do it?"

"Tish, I didn't do it. I didn't say it. I wasn't thinking it. I didn't put it in your mind."

"Well, I certainly didn't say it to myself."

I began to appreciate her confusion as the possibility dawned on me. I was almost equally flabbergasted. "If I didn't say it and you didn't say it," I asked, "then who does that leave?"

"How should I know?"

"All I was doing at the time was asking God to give you a blessing. I was asking hard."

"Are you suggesting it was God talking to me?"

"I don't know, but it seems to me a possibility."

Tish's face, previously stubborn, cynical and hard, despite its flabbiness, underwent a metamorphosis. She looked positively soft. "Why would God tell me I give Him pleasure?" she asked quietly. "I'm fat and ugly. And I'm not very nice. I'm self-centered and rude. I know I've been rude to you today. I don't mean to be, but it just comes out. Billy tells me I'm just trying to protect myself. So how could a fat bitch like me give God pleasure?"

"I don't know again," I answered. "I don't know how God thinks or feels. But I can guess because I know how I feel, and maybe He or She feels somewhat the same. I can tell you why you give *me* pleasure."

"Why?"

"I like watching people grow. I like watching all kinds of things: storms, snow falling, the grass turning green, flowers blooming, sunsets. But what gives me the most pleasure is watching people grow."

"How do you mean?"

"I know they don't push you here, and they probably don't even like to use the word 'progress,' but I don't know how else to explain it. I love to watch people make progress. When I first met you a week or so ago it seemed to me you were hopelessly stuck. But now it's clear you've made a lot of progress. To some extent that's been because of the way they've been treating you. The way your cripples' group is constructed is brilliant, and I really think they know what they're doing. But it's also because of the choices you've been making. You chose to go to group. You could have chosen to stay bored. I think Billy's right that your arrogance isn't so much rudeness as self-protection, but I wouldn't know what Billy said unless you told me, and you wouldn't have told me if you hadn't been listening to him. Maybe you don't buy it all yet but at least you've chosen to listen and to think about it a bit. I think you've been making a whole lot of good choices lately, and that pleases me. I rather imagine it pleases God too."

There was a long moment of silence between us. "I just can't believe that God actually talked to me," Tish said finally. "That God actually *would* talk to me!"

"I swear they weren't my words, so what other explanation could there be?"

"I dunno. I'll just have to think about it." Tish smiled as she continued, "I guess you could say I'll choose to think about it."

I smiled in turn. "And I think that would be a good choice," I said. "Why don't I leave you to it? I feel it's time for me to go back and do some thinking myself. Goodbye, Tish, and good luck."

"Goodbye," she responded, adding, "and thank you."

Back in my little green room I did indeed have some thinking to do. Insofar as she considered things at all, Tish was a rational, secular sort, so I had had to play her subtly. I'd largely let her come to the notion of an intervening God by herself. I'd spoken of it in terms of maybes, of possibilities and probabilities. But I knew perfectly well what had happened. God had spoken to Tish. Of that I had no doubt.

Perhaps several dozen times I'd heard that voice in my own head, the still small voice that is neither male nor female but both and more, the voice so full of surprises—and wisdom—that I knew it came from beyond me. No wonder that Tish had accused me of somehow creating it! Until she countenanced God she'd had no other recourse.

God had always spoken to me when I least expected it. Mind you, I'd prayed to hear that voice but those prayers had never seemed to be answered. At least not directly or on the spot. In fact, what had just transpired was the most direct and dramatic answer to a prayer I'd ever experienced. I'd prayed for Tish to receive a blessing from God, and that was exactly, precisely what had occurred. It was awesome.

What a perfect blessing for her! For anyone, but particularly for her. In this one respect I almost envied her. God had spoken words of wisdom yet never quite words of endearment to me. How I wished She or He might say to me, "You give me pleasure."

"I want to please You, Lord," I prayed. "Thank you for Tish. Thank you for answering my prayer. I guess at least my prayer pleased You. But do I please You otherwise? Will You let me know someday? Isabel has said that I will be coming home. Tomorrow? What will it be like? Most of the time You've seemed so far away for so long I don't feel worthy. I have so little faith in You. So little faith in myself. I'm sorry, Lord. Forgive me. Please. Please help me. I love You so much. Please bring me to You."

CHAPTER

13

As if understanding my eager-
ness, Isabel came for me early. "Are you ready?"

"Very much so," I answered, "but there are a couple of
things I think I should tell you about before we leave."

"Of course."

I recounted my previous day's experience with Tish. "I
don't know if you have any responsibility for her care, but
if you do I sure congratulate you. It's brilliant."

"No responsibility until she's ready to move on. But it so
happens I do know Billy, and I'll pass your compliments on
to him. Even here it's nice to be appreciated."

"I can't believe my prayer was answered," I continued.

"I can't believe otherwise," Isabel retorted. "It was a setup.
You set up the perfect opportunity for Him. There's no way
God would pass up an opportunity like that. And since we're
into compliments, it was pretty brilliant of you too, and I
rather imagine God's feeling grateful for it."

The notion that God might be grateful for me was so sweet

I could hardly bear it. But I wouldn't forget it. I tucked the thought away for future savoring.

I was not sure Isabel would be so complimentary when she heard how close I'd come to being thoroughly seduced by the mere illusion of a beautiful young woman's body. Nevertheless I fully described my encounter with Susan/Satan. To my surprise Isabel actually was laudatory again. "I thought it might well try to pull some trick on you," she commented. "Congratulations. You handled it well."

"I know this place is a combination of heaven, hell, and purgatory," I said, "but I seem to have been primarily in the heaven part. How is it that you let Satan hang around here?"

"Remember the Principle of Freedom?"

"Yes."

"Did you think it wouldn't apply to Satan? It's free to go wherever it wants."

"Maybe I'm stuck on earthly mythology," I acknowledged, "but I thought when Satan rebelled against God he or it was banished from heaven."

"Metaphorically, that's correct," Isabel responded. "God didn't banish it, however; it banished itself. Behave like that and no one in their right mind is going to want you around. Oh, it can hang around, but no decent soul's going to give it the time of day. It pulled out all the stops with you, and you still didn't buy it. If it came back would you trust it? No, you wouldn't even listen to it."

"You don't seem surprised it showed up," I commented. "I assumed the past two days were meant to be a time of preparation for me, and I gather a Satanic temptation must be a fairly standard part of the preparation."

"Yes and no," Isabel responded. "Yes, the two days are a

216

time for you to become truly certain that you're ready to move on. No, Satan's not a standard part of it."

"So not everyone gets tested?"

"Tested?" Isabel repeated, not understanding me for the first time.

"Yes, the way Satan tested me."

"You assume it was a test?"

"Wasn't it? I almost didn't pass."

Isabel laughed. "I suppose it was a test of sorts, but that wasn't Satan's intent; its intent was to divert you. The aim wasn't temptation for the sake of temptation but for the sake of diversion. A very good sign, actually."

Now it was my turn to be thoroughly confused. "A good sign? I don't understand."

"Satan's both desperate and understaffed," Isabel explained. "It's only got time to try to put out fires. It wouldn't have bothered with you unless you really represented a very great threat to it. It showed up when it did because it wanted to divert you from what you're intending to do. It didn't want you to be here when I came for you this morning. The committee for intercultural intervention may not prove to be the best place for you, but it's clear Satan doesn't want you to be there."

"That *is* a good sign," I agreed, finally comprehending.

I sensed the time had come. I'd told Isabel all that I'd needed. Wordlessly, I said goodbye to my little green room, knowing tonight I'd be sleeping in the void.

"No doubts?" Isabel asked.

I suddenly recalled how back on earth "the green room" was a name given to the small room in TV studios where performers waited before going out on stage. I had been in such rooms all too many times in order to publicize one of my books on some talk show or another. Usually they *were* green and not so unlike the color of this room I was leaving. I hated them. I'd hated doing publicity. I'd hated the artificiality of the shows. Above all, I'd hated the almost incapacitating terror I'd experienced in those rooms, not knowing what confusing, or even vicious, questions I might be asked and not knowing whether I would flub the answers. My own little green room here, my place prepared, had been a very different sort of place. But it occurred to me that in a real sense I was departing it now as if to go out on stage and perform.

"Of course I've got doubts," I answered Isabel. "And anxieties. At least a dozen, and I could probably cook up a hundred more if I set my mind to it. But that's me; I've always got doubts and anxieties, only the ones I've got now aren't worth the time of day. If you're ready, let's go."

She must have been ready because the very next thing I knew we were sitting together in the balcony of a grand auditorium. At least that's the best word I had for it since it was unlike any auditorium I'd seen on earth. It was completely round, with an empty round stage in the center. Otherwise, however, there seemed to be no ground floor or orchestra. Our balcony that entirely encircled the stage was steeply inclined. I could see no walls or ceiling. This had the effect of making the balcony seem suspended in midair. As there were no walls, there also were no doors, entrances, exits, aisles, or even chairs. Nor any visible lights, although somehow the balcony and stage were dimly lit while the gap between them was pitch black. Scattered throughout the balcony were souls like ourselves—"light balls" Tish would have called us—flickering slightly, and, even as I oriented myself, I was aware that more of us were appearing every minute.

I had two powerful impressions. Although all auditoriums are focused one way or another upon the stage, the focus of this one, with its steep, encircling balcony, was the most dramatic I'd ever seen. That empty stage was magically designed to capture our attention. The other, still stronger impression was of the design as a whole. While its lack of adornment was total, the building, if it could be called that, was somehow more elegant than any I'd been in before. It was a mystical space.

"Where are we?" I whispered.

"This is where the committee meets. You'll see the members starting to come on stage any moment now," Isabel replied.

"Who are the people in the balcony?"

"Many different types, not unlike at Congress in the United States. Some are tourists. Some are reporters, although they don't function at all like reporters back on earth. They're totally objective communicators who will report on this meeting to their own constituencies. They serve as liaisons. Others are scholars who analyze these meetings over time and serve the committee as consultants. Finally, there are the junior apprentices, like yourself, observing, learning, and occasionally participating or else available to be dispatched on some mission. You'll be spending a lot of time on this balcony."

A thought occurred to me. "Every space I've been in here thus far has more or less been prayed into existence. Is that also true of this auditorium?"

"Of course. Not by those here. They're here to concentrate

on the business at hand. But there's a committee of prayers right now creating this space. As soon as this meeting ends they'll be off duty until the next meeting. Until then this space won't exist."

I had a glimmer of the complexity of cooperation that must occur here. In some ways, things had seemed very simple. The Principle of Freedom governed everything. But think of my little green room! Think of this great hall. Think of Tish's cripples' group, with its one-to-one therapist-to-patient ratio. No, the society of heaven was not a simple matter at all.

My musing was interrupted by a flurry of activity. People—light balls—began appearing out of nowhere on the stage. They were in groups of two or three communicating among themselves quietly in a musical sort of way that I could neither understand nor distinctly hear. Since each little grouping was "speaking" at the same time, it was a gentle cacophony that reminded me of an orchestra tuning up before a performance. Soon there were more than fifty of them on the stage. At that point, one of the members of each group of three whisked from the stage to the balcony. As they crossed the black space between the stage and balcony their movement was like that of a meteor in the night sky. The remaining forty positioned themselves on the stage in an inner and outer circle of twenty each.

"The inner circle consists of the representatives," Isabel informed me. "The people in the outer one, right behind them, are their senior apprentices."

There was a long silence. Not a sound could be heard in the entire hall. The balcony audience seemed to be participating in it. It was the most intense silence I'd ever experienced.

Then out of the silence one of the representatives, a man, began to sing. I couldn't understand a word, and there was nothing spectacular about his voice. Nevertheless I was as enthralled as some people are by opera. His deep bass aria spoke to me of enormous sorrow and longing. It lasted for no more than a minute and the same silence returned.

It was perhaps another minute when a second representative started to sing—again a man but either a more lighthearted one or one with a more lighthearted message. Indeed, when he finished, everyone laughed: Isabel, everyone on stage, the whole balcony, except me, the only person there who did not understand the language.

The laughter subsided into deep silence again until a woman sang a song that seemed to embrace multiple mountain ranges and whole civilizations on the move across them. By now the singing had begun to remind me of fado, the almost lost art of the Portuguese troubadours who sang as no one else could, directly to the heart. No one else, that is, except these women and men who were far better and sent wave upon wave of chills up and down my spine.

During the next aria, Isabel whispered to me, "The woman who was singing before, the one whose light is more green than the others, is Isabel Morales—same first name as mine. She's going to be your boss, so to speak. She's the United States representative. Since she's Hispanic, she's got a particularly rich perspective on cultural issues. As does her senior apprentice. That's Jonathan Rhinehart, the man behind her whose light looks so steady. He's British, actually, but back on earth was a famed lecturer at the University of Edinburgh on American culture. You'll be the third member of the team."

I felt humbled. Much as I tried to focus on this pair who would be my superiors, however, I couldn't do so. The singing was too enthralling. As were the silences. In fact, it was the long, soft silences that finally clued me in on what was happening. Initially I'd been listening to arias, as if they were separate speeches punctuated by the silence, but gradually it dawned on me that they were a dialogue—not a dialogue between two but a whole group dialogue.

It was surprising I was so slow in coming to the realization, since back on earth I had been considered one of the world's experts on just such group interaction. No one knew better than I that a characteristic of unusually healthy group communication, one of the hallmarks of a true community, was these silences that indicated how deeply the participants were listening to each other, how they were taking the time to absorb what was being spoken and to contemplate its substance. In fact, I recalled Mary Martha telling me how all the committees here apparently functioned according to the principles of community and had been well trained to do so.

As soon as I realized all this, other realizations came tumbling after. The alterations in tone I was hearing were also indicative of a true community in action: the whole range of joy and sorrow, poetry and prose, anger and reconciliation, seriousness and humor, was being expressed. Nothing was being left out. All aspects were being considered. The group had a rhythm of its own and its members an exquisite sense of timing. It was a perfectly functioning organism. I exulted in the awareness that I was watching communicators who really knew what they were doing.

Shortly, I began to exult for additional reasons. Once I was aware that the group on stage was functioning as a true community, I started getting a dim sense of the drift of the dialogue. Although I did not know the language, it was so simultaneously emotional and precise that it was as if I could already follow it in my heart even if not my head. Moreover, because it obviously required more intuitive discipline than vocal skill, I had the sense that I would be able to learn it. And enjoy learning it. Isabel had been right.

Soon there was a change to the nature of the meeting. During the silences, people began streaking like meteors back and forth between stage and balcony. My guess at what was happening was confirmed by Isabel. "The senior apprentices are coming up here to dispatch the junior ones on mission and the consultants are moving down to offer suggestions to the representatives. The meeting has reached the stage of making decisions."

The flurry of activity was intermittent. It did not occur when the representatives were singing and happened only during certain silences. These flurries excited me. For the first time I had the impression not only that the representatives on stage were in community with each other but also with everyone in the balcony. It was now as if every person in the huge hall had become a component of the same giant, vibrating organism, an organism very much in action. It was beautiful.

The beauty reminded me of something I'd seen one place before. A favorite movie of mine back on earth had been *Close Encounters of a Third Kind* about meetings with extraterrestrials. The climax at the end of the movie came when an absolutely gigantic alien spaceship lands on earth at a predesignated spot to make actual friendly contact with humans. All over it lights were blinking and shifting. It was, for me, the best visual depiction of glory I'd ever seen. Until now.

I turned to Isabel. "Is this God?" I asked. "I feel as if I'm looking at God."

"You are," Isabel answered. "I think the most accurate way of putting it would be to say that what you are looking at is the surface of God. One surface, but the other surfaces are basically similar. Still, it's only the surface."

It was not long before the rhythm of the meeting shifted once again. The flurry of activity during the silences completely ceased, yet, if anything, the silences became more prolonged. The singing was quieter now and distinctly prayerful. I felt the meeting was winding down. Or was it winding up? Suddenly, all on stage, representatives and apprentices alike, sang at once in amazing harmony. It was a melodious shout of joy over in but a few seconds.

"This is where I leave you," Isabel announced. "Just wait here. Goodbye, Daniel. We all love you." And she was gone before I could even thank her.

The representatives and apprentices were commingling on stage, murmuring softly, saying their own goodbyes for the moment, I imagined. I was filled with anticipation and a feeling of privilege.

Then, when I least expected it, a light flashed from the stage meteorically through the blackness to my side. "I'm Jon," he said in clipped English. "All you need do is come with me." It was brief, almost curt, but somehow I had never felt more welcomed.

I went with him. My apprenticeship had begun.

ABOUT THE AUTHOR

M. Scott Peck, M.D., is a psychiatrist, management consultant, best-selling author, and a founder of the Foundation for Community Encouragement. He lives in northwestern Connecticut.